Ruth looked up, her face the color of plaster. "Hello, Jack." When she saw Bobby, tears began to roll down her face. "Bobby, I'm so glad you're here." She jammed a tissue under her nose. "I'm so sorry. I can't believe I'm unraveling like a loose hem. It's just so awful. A body, another one."

"It's okay, Aunt Ruth." Bobby hugged her tightly. "You're having a bad morning. Cry all you want. No one will blame you a bit."

"Well, Detective," Ellen Foots boomed. "What is going to become of our little town? Another body. It hasn't even been four months since the Fog Festival murder. I think it's connected to the film crew. That's what happens when you let new people in."

Other mysteries by Dana Mentink

Trouble Up Finny's Nose
Fog Over Finny's Nose

Don't miss out on any of our great mysteries. Contact us at the following address for information on our newest releases and club information:

Heartsong Presents—MYSTERIES! Readers' Service
PO Box 721
Uhrichsville, OH 44683
Web site: www.heartsongmysteries.com

Or for faster action, call 1-740-922-7280.

Treasure Under Finny's Nose

A Finny's Nose Mystery

Dana Mentink

HEARTSONG
PRESENTS
MYSTERIES

Dedication:

This book is dedicated to my two finest treasures, Emily and Holly. I thank God on bended knee for entrusting me with His precious angels.

ISBN 978-1-60260-163-5

Scripture taken from the King James Version of the Bible.

Scripture taken from the HOLY BIBLE, NEW INTERNATIONAL VERSION®. NIV®. Copyright © 1973, 1978, 1984 by International Bible Society. Used by permission of Zondervan. All rights reserved.

All of the characters and events in this book are fictitious. Any resemblance to actual persons, living or dead, or to actual events is purely coincidental.

Cover design: Kirk DouPonce, DogEared Design
Cover illustration: Jody Williams

Our mission is to publish and distribute inspirational products offering exceptional value and biblical encouragement to the masses.

Printed in the U.S.A.

"Your ship went down in a violent storm. You've spent three days clinging to the wreckage, watching the people around you die from exposure and exhaustion. You finally struggle to shore and collapse there, unconscious until the sun warms your body, easing you back to life. What is the first thought that fills your head when you open your eyes?"

Ethan Ping leaned forward in anticipation.

Ruth Budge heaved a sigh. "I want Milk Duds." She felt only a sliver of guilt as Ethan, her director, slapped his clipboard against his thigh. The man couldn't be more than twenty-two and a college student to boot. How could he understand a forty-eight-year-old pregnant woman? Come to think about it, how could she? The only thing she knew for certain was if she didn't get some Milk Duds soon, she was going to have to put the director in a half nelson. Re-enacting the life of the indomitable Indigo Orson could wait. She was a desperate woman.

Ethan continued to stare at her in exasperation, the leaves of the oak behind him silhouetting his dark hair in green. His slender eyebrows drew together in a single line above his almond-shaped eyes. "Mrs. Budge, I know you are having a bit of trouble concentrating."

He didn't know the half of it. She was pregnant and just months away from her forty-ninth, yes, forty-ninth, birthday. If her life were a novel it would be ridiculously improbable. She might very well be the oldest known mother in the Western Hemisphere. Then a kick from somewhere in the vicinity of her kidney reminded her that it was all too real. Ignoring the heartburn that plagued her regardless of what she ate, she tried to listen to the young filmmaker.

"We've got a deadline on this reenactment project, Mrs. Budge. It has to be finished by the end of June, or we're not going to make our deadline. I don't mean to pressure you or anything, but Reggie here needs to get the footage."

Reggie, a tall man with cocoa skin, waved at her. He rested the giant camera on his shoulder as if it weighed nothing at all.

She waved back and resisted the urge to curl up on the ground where she stood for a nap.

Sandra Marconi, a chubby blonde with her arms full of binders, interrupted. "Maybe Mrs. Budge just needs a little break, Ethan. Ruth, why don't you go sit in the sun for a minute."

Ruth didn't need a second invitation. The spasm in her back was working its way up her spine and into her shoulder blades. She eased onto a lawn chair that sat in a precious spot of early summer sun and closed her eyes. The warmth lulled her into a comfortable haze until the sound of a bell startled her.

Alva Hernandez wobbled up the path. He rang the bicycle bell again before he dismounted and hobbled over, a red toolbox in his gnarled hand. "Hello, sweet cheeks. What's shakin'?"

"Hello, Alva. Did you help Monk load up?" Monk, her husband of almost two years, had reluctantly left on a trip to care for his ailing father. She hoped it was reluctantly, though with the state of their house and her propensity to burst into tears every five minutes, maybe he viewed it as a respite. He was a patient man, but she knew sometimes he was at a complete loss about how to handle her kaleidoscoping emotions. She really couldn't help him with it as she was confounded by her emotional state herself.

"Yup, I helped your hubby stow his gear." Alva shoved his stringy white hair out of his eyes. "He's off to the airport. He assigned me a mission 'fore he left, though. I ain't had a mission since Korea." His filmy eyes sparkled. "Ain't that something?"

Ruth smiled at the enthusiastic octogenarian. "What's the mission, Alva?"

He started. "Oh yeah. I'm to be your, what's it called again? Oh yeah. Your ninny."

"My what?"

"Ninny. No, that don't sound right." He scratched his chin. "Give me a second here. Oh, right. Nanny, not ninny. I'm to take care of you and the little bun in your oven until Monk gets back. I'm to help you with the birds and make sure you get enough food and all that. Help you tie your shoes iffen the baby swells you up too big and the like. Stuff like that."

Ruth suppressed a groan. Alva was indeed a help with her crabby flock of disabled seagulls, and he often lent a hand tracking down an AWOL bird. The man was half a bubble off plumb, but he was devoted to her. Still, she really just wanted to climb in a hole and disappear. The thought of having a personal attendant until Monk returned didn't appeal to her at all.

Alva set the toolbox on the ground and snapped open the lid. It was crammed to the brim with candy. "I put me together a survival kit. Whatcha want? Kisses? Chocolate bar? Tootsie Rolls? The peanut butter cups is squashed so they ain't good anymore. How about a package of gumdrops?"

Ruth's spirits picked up. "You don't possibly have any Milk Duds in there, do you?"

He foraged around in the bottom. "Aha. There you are, sweet cheeks. I said I'd take care of you, didn't I?"

Ruth mentally retracted any unenthusiastic thoughts about Alva's nannying. "Thank you, Alva. You are a lifesaver."

He cocked his head and began to rummage in the box again. "You want a Lifesaver? I got them, too. Cherry, butterscotch, them purple-colored ones. . ."

"I'm fine with these, Alva." She tore open the package and ate greedily.

Sandra squeezed into the chair next to Ruth. "I'm sorry about Ethan. He's really a brilliant guy, but he's driven, so delays make him crazy."

Ruth sighed. "I don't mean to criticize, but why did you ask me to do this reenactment business anyway? I mean, for one thing I'm not Hispanic and I'm not an actor. I'm just a vermiculturist."

"What's that?"

"A worm farmer," Alva piped up. He offered a bag to the woman. "Candy corns?"

"Uh, no thanks. Well, as you know, this is the anniversary of the wreck of the *Triton* right off the coast there. At least that's what our research lends us to believe." She pointed down the slope to the foam-capped ocean. "Our project is to take a photographic record of the wreck, but

Ethan thought adding a dramatic reenactment would punch up the human interest element."

"I agree," Ruth said, "but why don't you get a real actor?"

Sandra twiddled with the binder. "Because you have to pay real actors, and our budget is stretched as it is with the underwater photography gear. We've got every available dime invested in this project, believe me, and there's just no wiggle room. Besides, your public relations gal told us how versatile you were."

Ruth coughed. "My what?"

"Tiny lady with a loud voice. Maude something." Sandra snapped her fingers. "Maude Stone, I think it is. She found out we were coming to Finny and contacted us to see how she could be involved. We told her we needed an actor. She suggested herself at first, but we didn't think that would work since her leg is in a cast."

"As soon as I get hold of her, she's going to need a cast for the other leg," Ruth grumbled.

"Pardon?"

"Never mind."

A bird swooped overhead and headed toward the water. The women looked up into the brilliant blue sky over the ocean. A small boat bobbed in the water. Ruth could just make out the banana yellow cap of Roxie Trotter, a relative newcomer to the town. The wind picked up, toying with the oak branches above their heads.

"Do you get many tourists in June?" Sandra asked.

"Some, but fall is better weather-wise because there is much less fog." Ruth pointed to Roxie's boat. "Roxie started up a fishing tour business a year ago. She said her business booms in the fall."

Sandra tipped her face to the sun. "It is beautiful in Finny right now. The vegetation is so lush, almost tropical. Once the fog burns off, everything sort of puts on these dazzling colors."

"Yes, it is nice here." Ruth inhaled the tang of salt air. "Even in the winter you can still find good weather in northern California. From the top of Finny's Nose, you can see all the way to the Farralon Islands when it's clear."

She had a sudden flashback to standing on top of the mountain three months back, when the pieces of a murderous puzzle fell into place. She shuddered, reburying the memories of that awful time back where they belonged.

Sandra laughed, gazing at the vibrant green outline of the tall peak. "I've never stood at the top of a nose before. You're right. The thing really does look just like a nose."

"If you look at it upside down, it's the spittin' image of Richard Nixon," Alva added, around a mouthful of candy.

Sandra gave him an incredulous look.

Ruth could only shrug at her.

Reggie took the camera off his shoulder and sauntered over. "Hey, ladies. We've lost the light for today. We'll have to pick it up tomorrow."

Ruth tried to look disappointed, but her feet were shouting a silent *yippee!*

Sandra handed her a binder. "Why don't you read up on Indigo tonight? I think you'll find her inspiring. I'll see you tomorrow, Mrs. Budge."

Ruth finished her candy and took her nanny's arm.

The comforting smell of furniture polish greeted her back

at the cottage. In spite of the emptiness she felt at Monk's absence, she was relieved to be home. After making her way carefully around the piles of sheetrock left by Carson the contractor, Monk's crazy Italian bowling buddy, Ruth snuggled on the sofa with a cup of tea. She opened the binder and read the prologue.

> *Isabela Ortiz was a Mexican servant in the house of Mr. Edward Orson. She accompanied them on a steamship which departed from New York in 1851 en route to San Francisco. The ship was overloaded with coal, and only fifty passengers were on board when the ship collided with another steamer, which sustained only minor damage. There were twelve reported survivors of the* Triton *passengers and crew. Eleven were picked up six miles south when the tide carried them to a rocky outcropping. Isabela, separated from the other survivors, made it to shore in a different location. Fearing persecution from the white miners, she took the name Indigo Orson and lived as a man.*

Imagine, Ruth thought. Surviving a wreck, washing ashore, and assuming a new identity. She pictured the Finny shoreline, rugged, cold, inhospitable for much of the time. Isabel was indeed a force to be reckoned with to have carved out a life here. She skimmed the first few pages until a photocopied passage caught her eye. The script was loopy and hard to read even when she held it to the light.

Why am I alive? I can only think it to be the grace of God. He must have His own plan, to save me, a worthless servant, and let the others die. It is a miracle to have my tiny book and stub of pencil to write with. The ship broke like an old matchstick with a terrible groaning sound. Señor Orson was crushed by falling wood, lifted in a mighty wave. He looked surprised when the beam hit him. All his money couldn't do him any help then. Down he went, the waves swallowed him up as if he'd never existed.

Señora Orson and I clung to a piece of wreckage. She looked so lost, poor niña. I tried to comfort her, but she never had an idea how to take care of herself, that's why she had me along on the trip. She could not understand that her husband had been killed right before her very eyes.

I knew from the moment Señor Orson determined to sail to San Francisco with his precious box that we would be thrown into trouble. And so desperate he was to go that he booked passage on this coal-filled tub. Why oh why couldn't he have waited until a right proper ship was available? It was a doomed trip from the very start, and Señor paid a terrible price in more ways than one.

Poor Señora Orson. After the boat cracked into pieces, she just kept on asking if it was safe. When will we get home, she asked over and over. I looked out at the terrible wide ocean and all the poor dead folks floating like corks around us. I felt the tug of the current and the whack of the sea creatures that

would touch my legs where they dangled in the
water. What did it matter then? It was all in God's
hands and He cares little for treasure.

Treasure? What kind of riches would have caused
Orson to risk it all and take passage on the coal ship?

The phone rang. Ruth jumped.

"Hello, gorgeous. How are you?" Monk's voice boomed
across the line.

"I'm not gorgeous. I'm big and fat, and I have eaten
my body weight in candy today."

"Now, none of that kind of talk. You're always
beautiful to me. Did Alva help you with the birds?"

"Yes. They're all fed and tucked in for the night."

"How's the drywall repair coming along?"

"I only know Carson's been here because there's a
gaping hole in the baby's room and a pile of sheetrock in
the middle of the living room floor."

He snorted. "Who would think termites could cause
so much damage?"

"Carson could give them a run for their money. How
is your father?"

"He's on the mend. Doctors say he'll be home in a
few days. That means I will, too. I can't wait to get back
to you."

She felt trembly inside. "Is that really true, Monk?
Even though I am the oldest expectant mother on the
planet?" *And the one child I had decades ago is a virtual
stranger?* She pushed the thought away.

"Listen to me, Ruthy. You're my darling. I don't know
why the good Lord decided to put us up to this parenting

thing so late in the game, but He knows what He's doing. I love you and we'll face everything together."

She could picture him there, his giant hands cradling the phone, his eyes warm and gentle. "I love you, Monk," she said softly.

"I love you, too, Ruthy. You just give Junior a pat for me, and I'll call you again tomorrow."

"Okay. I'll pat somewhere around my pancreas. I think that's where Junior is wedged right now."

His laugh echoed in her ears as she hung up and headed for bed.

Though her body was steeped in fatigue, she could not get to sleep. Every time she found a comfortable position, she'd feel a strange flutter of movement. Maybe it was gas, as everyone seemed to believe. The infant was barely three months along, so how had it managed to expand her waistline and grow big enough for her to feel it so distinctly? She remembered an old black and white horror movie about a woman who had given birth to an octopus-like creature that immediately set out to conquer planet earth. She hoped this child would at least fix the sheetrock before he or she embarked on world domination.

Finally, somewhere after two a.m. she got up and fixed herself more tea. She looked out of the front window toward the inlet where Indigo's ship had foundered so many years ago. Was it a dark night like this when Isabel found herself in the sea? Was there only a sliver of moon to light the way to shore?

Ruth started to put down her cup to return to bed when she saw it.

A tiny flicker of light, dancing under the waves like a fallen star.

2

Ruth steeled her stomach as she sprinkled scraps on the worm bed. In the pre-dawn gloom she watched the surface of the soil undulate with happy wiggling bodies. She tried not to inhale the scent of vegetable peelings and loamy soil. The standing monthly order at Pete's Fish and Tackle had to be filled whether she was nauseated or not. The birds rustled and squawked from their pen in the corner of the yard. She counted eleven beaks. It was always a relief to know that they were all present. Not too long ago poor Ulysses was mutilated by a deranged killer looking to send a message to Ruth. The bird hadn't survived, and she still looked for his fuzzy head in the gaggle.

The feathered brood was founded by her late husband, Philip, who just couldn't stand to euthanize the numerous avian victims brought to his veterinary office, and since they were unable to fly, there was no hope of releasing them. He named them all after U.S. presidents, except for Martha, who was the first lady of the bunch.

Grover pushed his way to the gate and inclined his pearly head for a scratch. He was knocked aside by the larger Milton, who flapped his white wings and gave her a "Where is my breakfast?" honk.

"You don't get your breakfast until I get mine, you greedy bird. Then we'll go for a walk, if you can behave." After a virtually sleepless night, she wondered how she would find the energy to walk.

Her breakfast, as it turned out, was dry toast and decaf

coffee. She had doubts that even that simple meal would stay where she put it. With grim determination, she donned her warm jacket with the ever-present bag of corn chips in the pocket and went outside to gather the squadron.

The morning air was chilly, but the fog that huddled along the ground was scant. It would burn off by early afternoon. June really was a good time to come to Finny, she thought as she headed through town. After the cool of morning, the afternoon would no doubt shape up to be lovely. A glorious scent of cinnamon from the Buns Up Bakery signaled the start of Al's morning preparations. She waved a hello to Luis Puzan as he cleaned the windows of his grocery store. A light shone in the top floor of the Finny Hotel.

"I wonder if Ethan is up doing some work on his script?" It was a good place for creativity. The bougainvillea was vibrant against the peeling white paint of the old inn. In the distance, patrons could see the wild Pacific, wind tossed and shadowed by the enormous beds of kelp that undulated under the surface. The building was slightly ramshackle, but the view couldn't be beat.

She scooped Rutherford out of the fountain in the center of town square. Even close to two years later she couldn't forget the day she and Alva pulled a slippery body from that bubbling water. The nausea returned with a vengeance. She took several deep breaths and sniffed the orange peel Flo Hodges insisted would drive away the worst morning sickness.

A cheerful bicycle bell announced the arrival of her erstwhile guardian. Alva coasted to a perilous stop, weaving his way in and out of birds, dinging his bicycle bell to startle them out of the way with very little effect. "Morning, sweet cheeks. Monk told me to check every day and see if you done ate your vitamins." He took a battered notebook and a pencil stub out of his jacket pocket.

"Yes, Alva, I did take my vitamins, and so far I haven't thrown them up."

He scribbled a note. "Saturday. Seven o'clock. Took pills. No throw up. Got it." The pencil stuck out at a jaunty angle after he put it behind his ear. "Where are we going today?"

She tucked the flyaway hair that was riddled with ever more gray strands behind her ears. "I thought I'd take the birds for a walk down to the beach before rehearsal. I saw a strange light in the water last night. I can't get it out of my mind."

His white eyebrows shot up. "Strange? You figure maybe it's a sea monster or something? You know I saw that Loch Ness creature swimmin' in Tookie Newsome's trout pond last spring. I betcha he relocated to the ocean on account of he needed more leg room."

Ruth suppressed a giggle. "Could be. Tookie's pond is a bit small for a sea monster. Did you finish your route?" Alva was probably the oldest newspaper delivery boy in the country, but he did his job with meticulous care.

"Sure. I got up extra early so's I could report for bird walking duty." He opened the tool box and handed her some Milk Duds.

She patted his arm. Ignoring the fact that her waist was expanding with every passing minute, she opened the package.

A tiny, black-haired woman with an ankle cast hobbled

over, her arms full of grocery bags.

Ruth's eyes narrowed. "Good morning, Maude. I understand I've got you to thank for being roped into this acting job."

Maude shot a poisonous look at Alva before giving Ruth her full attention. "Well, I would have been happy to take on the role myself, but they said the cast was a problem. I really can't see why they couldn't shoot from the waist up. Of course, if somebody hadn't left their inflatable raft on the steps of the Dr. Soloski's office, I never would have broken my foot in the first place."

Alva crossed his arms. "How many times do I gotta say it? I told you that tweren't my raft. I dunno how it got there. You can't pin that on me."

Alva and Maude had a long-standing feud that began when she accused Alva of stomping on her primroses while he delivered the newspaper. Though Maude tried everything, even videotaping, to catch Alva in the act, she had never found proof of intentional wrongdoing.

The wind whipped Maude's hair into a wild tangle. "Well, you were there for a cleaning, weren't you? Even though you don't have any real teeth left."

"I do so have teeth, lots of 'em, the real kind and the plastic kind. Fer yer information, Doc says I gotta have a cavity filled in my back mortar."

"That's molar, you idiot." Maude was distracted by the crinkle of Ruth's candy bag. "What are you doing eating candy at this hour?" Her glance shot to Alva. "Did you give her that?"

He straightened up. "It just so happens, I'm her nanny. It's my job."

"You're not a nanny, you're a nincompoop. A woman in her condition, especially at her age, should not be eating candy."

Alva folded his arms. "She's gonna have anything she wants while the bun is in the oven. Monk said so. I'm keeping a report for him. I'm in charge."

Ruth noticed the flush mounting across the woman's cheeks. She hastened to intervene. "Maude, what are all the bags for?"

"I'm making boxed lunches for the first tour group."

"What tour group?"

"I've sold twelve tickets to the Women's Literary League of Half Moon Bay. They're coming to visit the film site. You can meet them later. I'm providing lunch and a comprehensive informational tour. I've got another group lined up, too. A few more weeks of this and we might be able to buy that copy machine for F.L.O.P."

F.L.O.P. was the Finny Ladies Organization for Preparedness. With Maude at the helm, they were prepared for anything, from quakes to quarantines. "You're giving tours of the film site? Did you run this by the director?"

"Oh, please. He doesn't dictate what goes on in Finny. He might be inspired to greater artistic heights, having a real audience there." She shifted the bags and leaned closer, peering at Ruth's face. "Why don't you ask the crew about some stage makeup? You look all waxy and there are some sun spots on your cheeks that could stand to be concealed. Do you have your lines memorized yet?"

Ruth moved her waxy, spotted face away from Maude. "Not yet. I'm working on it."

Alva wrote in his notebook.

"What are you doing?" Maude demanded.

"I'm adding to my report. Saturday. Seven thirty. Heading to the beach. Interrupted by old bat with a sack full of groceries."

Maude's lips parted in fury.

"Uh, we've really got to go walk the birds before rehearsal." Ruth grabbed Alva's arm. "Come on, let's hurry. Bye now." She moved off as fast as her thickened middle would allow. They headed down slope to the beach.

The morning chill held the fragrance of cypress and cedar. Gravel crunched underfoot as they walked, the birds milling in a noisy crowd around them. She felt a sudden onslaught of self-pity. "Alva, do you think I look waxy?"

He looked closely at her face. "Nah. You're a real looker, Ruth. Your face is all plump and shiny. The best women are like doughnuts, you know, round and glazed."

They lapsed into silence as Ruth tried to digest Alva's wisdom. Round and glazed. Neither sounded particularly attractive. She was overwhelmed by a pang of loneliness. Not just for Monk. She desperately missed her friend Dimple and Dimple's daughter, Cootchie. Cootchie had been a part of Ruth's soul since she had stepped in to raise her when Dimple's lover was killed. At times, when Ruth pleaded with God to help her be a good mother to her unborn child, He sent her a tender memory of Cootchie. It was as if He said, "You love Cootchie, and you'll love this child, too."

Another voice spoke up, with different words. *You loved Bryce with every ounce of your being, and he won't give you the time of day. And look what happened to Cootchie, kidnapped while in your care. Now she's living with her real grandma in Arizona.*

Ruth silenced the thoughts with a strengthening prayer. She might be waxy, round, and glazed, but she still had enough strength to pray.

They made it down to the rugged stretch of beach, the wind fighting them along the way. A crooked line of rocks dotted the gravelly sand and joined up to form a black cliff in the distance.

The birds swarmed back and forth, playing tag with the waves. They kept away from the few able-bodied birds that poked in the sand. It made her sad that her birds knew instinctively that they were not part of that wild flock anymore. She wondered if they felt a pang when they saw their uninjured brothers fly away on graceful wings. Did they realize they were forever earthbound?

She walked carefully around the slick boulders, keeping an eye on Franklin. He was her delicate bird, after losing an eye and a foot to a cat. The vet had fashioned him a little plastic tube that slipped on his leg to protect his stump and help with balance. He despised having the contraption put on, but it helped him keep up or at least out of the way of the others.

Looking back, she saw Alva with his plastic shovel, digging for treasure. The image brought back the words of Isabel Ortiz. As she watched the gray waves scour the sand, she wondered what it had been like for the servant woman to cling to the wreckage and watch the people die all around her. All those people and their possessions, lost to the arms of an angry ocean.

Franklin hobbled ahead and disappeared around yet another jagged rock.

"Don't go too far," Ruth scolded. "I'm in no position

to attempt a water rescue."

She edged around the obstruction.

Franklin poked his slender beak in a pile of slippery black kelp.

Ruth took another glance at the oddly shaped mound of seaweed.

Her mouth went dry.

"Alva," she called in a shaky voice. "Can you come here for a second?"

He trotted over, still holding onto the bucket. "Good news. I found a can opener. Ain't that handy? You just never know when you're gonna need a can opener. It don't seem hardly rusted at all. Wonder why someone threw it away?"

She pointed. "Take a look over there, Alva. Is that what I think it is?"

The old man squinted, mashing a fist into his eyes before he peered again. "Well, would you look at that. It ain't no sea monster." He patted his pockets.

Ruth fought hard against the bile that rose in her throat. It took all her strength of will to contain the scream that coalesced inside her. After a moment, she got her vocal cords to cooperate. "Alva, I think you better call the police."

"Who, me? I ain't got a phone, sweet cheeks." He found the pencil and notebook. "I gotta add this to my report." He licked the pencil point and began to write with relish. "Saturday. Seven fifty-five. We found ourselves a body."

3

Jack Denny tried again to get out of the police car, and again he stopped with his hand on the door. There must be some paperwork to be done, an arrest report or neighbor complaint that needed to be addressed, that would take him away from this location. He stared down at the cell phone clipped to his belt. It remained stubbornly silent. The irony.

"Man, Jack," he mumbled to his stubbled chin in the rearview mirror, "you are losing it, fella." That was only partially true. He'd already lost it the moment he'd laid eyes on Bobby, right before she'd flattened an obnoxious assailant twice her size. She had been gone from Finny for two months but had returned to run her uncle Monk's business while he was away tending to his father.

Yes, Bobby was back, and Jack was alternately terrified and elated.

He stood outside Monk's Coffee and Catering with sweating palms and his stomach in knots. It was ridiculous. He could deal with homicides and mobsters, so why did this woman make his heart hop around like a wild rabbit? Jack took a gulp of air and headed toward the shop. He made it almost to the front door before he stopped again.

Maybe Bobby had met someone. She had been away long enough. She was an attractive, educated, intriguing woman, and a park ranger to boot. Maybe she'd met some outdoorsy type who wasn't afraid to take on a relationship, a man who didn't fear losing everything. The thought sent a stab of ice through his gut.

The windows were dim. Bobby must not be opening up the shop today. With a surge of relief, Jack reached for his keys to head back to the station.

"Are you admiring Uncle Monk's new paint?"

He whirled around and dropped the keys.

Bobby looked at him with her head cocked, black eyes sparkling under a fringe of bangs. She hardly came up to his chin, but her eyes had such power and strength.

"I, uh, no, not really, no." He picked up the keys and felt a flood of heat to his face. "I heard you were back."

"Word travels fast in Finny. I was taking out the trash and I saw your car. Do you want to come in for some coffee?"

He sighed. "I would love to."

They walked into the shop. Bobby prepared the coffee and filled heavy mugs. The two settled into battered chairs by the window. In the distance, the ocean performed acrobatics under a delicate layer of fog. Jack sipped the strong brew and tried to calm his pattering heart. "When did you get in?"

"Just this morning. I haven't even seen Aunt Ruth yet. Uncle Monk asked me to keep the coffee and muffin business open and take catering orders. He's hoping to be back next week. It killed him that he had to go."

"It's great that you could help out. Ruth has her hands full right now. Maude's already got her doing some photo documentary thing and an acting job." He cleared his throat. It was time to ask the question that kept him awake at night. "Have you decided on a job?"

"I've been looking at some positions in Arizona, and one in California, plus the spot that's up for grabs in Utah.

They all have their good points, but I haven't made any decisions yet."

"I see." Jack's thoughts ran wild. *Pick the one in California. Stay here, close to me. Please.* He wasn't sure which scared him more, the thought of her leaving or the thought of her staying.

She put down her mug. "So how have you been? How's Paul?"

"He's great. The doctor is really pleased with his progress."

"Is he talking more then?"

"Not as much as he did when you were around."

Paul had been selectively mute since he saw his mother die suddenly when he was two. Now, at age five, he was just starting to string words together. Paul and Bobby spent hours building Lego spaceships, and Jack spent hours watching them, afraid to break the spell. "He misses Cootchie, too. We're all hoping she comes back this summer."

The conversation died away. He found himself watching her, staring at her as if he was trying to memorize every detail of her face. When the silence became awkward, he cleared his throat. "Nate told me to ask you how to get a Barbie shoe out of his pencil sharpener."

She laughed, high and musical. "Did the triplets get him again?"

He nodded. "I keep telling him not to fall asleep in the recliner. Cunning little stinkers. You'd think a cop wouldn't be so easy to ambush, but he sleeps like the dead."

"Well, I can't help with the Barbie thing, I never played with them. I was more of a Tinkertoy kind of gal."

He put down his empty cup and his fingers brushed

her arm. Without thinking, he covered her hand with his. "I missed you."

She squeezed his hand before pulling away to gently straighten the collar of his plaid shirt.

His breath caught at the feel of her soft touch on his skin. He wanted nothing more than to pull her into his arms and never let her go.

She opened her mouth to speak when the chirp of his phone interrupted.

Suppressing a groan, he answered it. Bobby took their mugs to the kitchen while he talked. After a minute he hung up. "You are not going to believe this, but Ruth found a body on the beach."

Her eyes widened. "Oh no. Who is it? Is she okay?"

"I don't know, but maybe you'd better come along with me. She may need support."

"I got your back, Detective."

He should be so lucky.

⸺

Jack drove code three down the bumpy trail to the beach. Bobby didn't seem to mind the jostling. As a matter of fact, she looked as energized as he felt. Cold air rushed in through the open windows, and her cheeks pinked under her swirling cap of short black hair.

Alva met them at the top of the bluff. His eyes were enormous in his shrunken face. "Right down there, Detective. Howdy, Miss Walker. You come to check out the body? I been keeping the folks back. I sent Roxie away, but that busybody Ellen Foots is here with Dr. Soloski. I told 'em to keep off on account of they could smudge the evidence or something, but you can't tell Ellen nothing. She's as bad as Maude. You may just hafta arrest her for construction of justice or something."

Jack nodded. "Thanks, Alva. Let's go have a look."

They made their way down the windy path to the beach. Ruth sat on a boulder, amidst a swarm of seagulls. Ellen stood next to her, her six-foot-four frame towering over a slender man who completed the trio.

Officer Nathan Katz knelt next to a slick heap several yards away, taking pictures. He looked up and nodded. Jack and Bobby hastened over to the group.

Ruth looked up, her face the color of plaster. "Hello, Jack." When she saw Bobby, tears began to roll down her face. "Bobby, I'm so glad you're here." She jammed a tissue under her nose. "I'm so sorry. I can't believe I'm unraveling like a loose hem. It's just so awful. A body, another one."

"It's okay, Aunt Ruth." Bobby hugged her tightly. "You're having a bad morning. Cry all you want. No one will blame you a bit."

"Well, Detective," Ellen Foots boomed. "What is going to become of our little town? Another body. It hasn't even been four months since the Fog Festival murder. I think it's connected to the film crew. That's what happens when you let new people in." She turned wide eyes on the man next to her. "Oh, not you, of course, Gene. We are so lucky to have a dentist here." She squeezed his arm.

The sandy-haired man winced under the pressure of Ellen's assertive gesture. "Detective, I'm relieved you're here. I took a look to see if there was any need for resuscitation, but there, er, wasn't."

Jack thought the poor guy looked as green around the gills as Ruth, but that might be attributed to the attention of the ferocious librarian. "Thanks, Doctor. I'll need to talk to you both in a few minutes." He put a hand on Ruth's shoulder. "Are you all right?"

She nodded, balling up another Kleenex. "Yes. You'd think, seeing as how this is the second body Alva and I have happened upon, I wouldn't be such a mess. It must be the baby."

"Don't worry about it. Baby or no, finding a dead person is not something anybody takes in stride." He and Bobby exchanged a glance, and she sat down next to her aunt. "Sit tight. I'll be back in a minute."

Jack did a slow circle around the body. The stiff figure was sizable, clad in a dive suit, complete with air tanks that lay half buried in the sand. The body lay face up, eyes closed. Jack looked at the ocean for a moment to clear his brain.

Nate was down on one knee, taking a close-up of the dead man's head. The damp sand made a wet patch on his pants where he knelt.

"Whatcha got, Nate?"

"Ruth said his name was Reggie. He was a cameraman for the film crew. Big guy, good diving gear. He's been dead awhile." Nate huffed into his lush mustache. "His mask is missing, but I don't see much sign of trauma. Wasn't shark chow, I don't think. Coroner is on his way."

Jack raised an eyebrow. "You know you have the word *Daddy* written in magic marker on the side of your neck?"

He nodded. "I know. I told Maddie we need to send them to a convent, but she says they don't take six-year-olds, especially triplets."

"At least they can spell Daddy right. That's a good sign."

"Yeah." Nate stood up and brushed the sand from his hands. "Is that Bobby over there?"

"I was at Monk's when I got the call. She came along to give Ruth some help."

Nate shot him a sidelong glance. "Is she staying in Finny for a while this time?"

"Maybe. So what's your take on this? Diving accident?"

Nate sneezed and blew his nose on an enormous handkerchief he pulled from his pocket. "Could be. But why would the guy dive at night anyway?"

Jack watched a bird swoop down to investigate and flutter away again. "I know they've been filming the wreck. Do you suppose they decided to get some night footage?"

Nate shook his head. "In these waters? By himself? That's gotta break every rule in the safe diving handbook."

They stared for another few minutes. Jack sighed. "I'm going to talk to Ruth and Alva again."

Nate readied his camera and went back to work.

The old man was sitting by a red toolbox when Jack returned. "Tell me how you and Ruth found the body, Alva."

He scratched his wrinkled forehead. "We're walkin' the birds, ya see, me and Ruth. Then I find this here can opener in the sand. Don't that just beat it? That's a lucky find, I'll tell you, and hardly any rust."

"Okay, you were walking the birds and you found a can opener. What next?"

"Sweet cheeks calls me over to see the sea monster. Only it ain't no sea monster, it's a dead guy. I don't have no phone so I run back to town and Bubby calls it in." His face darkened. "Ellen heard me 'splaining it to Bubby and she and the doctor headed down. I been tryin' to lay low on account of the fact that I need to get my mortar drilled and filled. I'm not too keen on the idea." He continued to rummage in the toolbox.

Jack smiled. "Did you know the dead man, Alva?"

"Nah, never met him. Just saw him at the film site a couple of times. Never said more than a 'good morning' to him." He straightened up. "Aha! Here it is, Ruthy honey. I told you Alva was gonna take care of ya." He handed her a crumpled bag of Milk Duds.

Ruth gave him a wan smile. "Thank you, Alva. You are so good to me."

Jack waited until she ate a few candies. A tiny stain of color returned to her pale cheeks. "Did you want to add anything to Alva's statement?"

She closed her eyes for a moment. "Yes," she said, as she opened them. "The reason we came to the beach in the first place. Last night I got up around two, I think, and I looked out my front window. I saw a light, far out in the water. It almost seemed like it was under the water, but I couldn't be sure. Do you think I imagined it? I am under the influence of rampant hormones at the moment. I can't remember my name half the time."

He chuckled. "I don't think you imagined it. The victim was diving at night for some reason we can't figure right now. You might have seen his light. Two o'clock you say?"

"Somewhere around there."

Gene Soloski's forehead creased as he and Ellen approached. "Not my business, of course, but it seems pretty ridiculous to dive at night in these waters, especially alone."

"I agree." Ellen patted the dentist on the back. "Do you dive, Doctor?"

"No, ma'am. I'm a land creature all the way."

Ellen smiled coquettishly. "Except for your days as a tree doctor."

"I guess I traded in the bark for the bite."

Ellen exploded into loud guffaws. The librarian's wild mane of hair vibrated along with the laughter. "You're just a stitch, Gene."

"And they say dentists don't have a sense of humor." Dr. Soloski spotted Alva, crouched behind Ruth. "There you are. I've been leaving messages with Mrs. Hodges for you all week. Don't forget your appointment on Monday morning, Mr. Hernandez. We've got to get that tooth fixed before you wind up with an abscess."

Alva's brows drew together. "I think I got me some other appointment on Monday. Could be I got a Boy Scout meeting that day."

"Cancel it." Ellen didn't take her eyes off the dentist.

Alva's face crimped. "I don't got a ride to the office, and this leg's been bothering me. Too far to walk."

"I can take you, Alva." Ruth patted his shoulder. "I'll stay with you, too. It will be okay."

"There, you see?" The doctor smiled. "It won't hurt a bit, I promise."

"Yeah, yeah," Alva grumbled. "I bet that's what they said to that Marie Antoinette broad, too."

Jack finished scribbling in his notebook. "Okay, I think we're done for now. I'll be talking to each of you again, soon."

"All right." Dr. Soloski took a last glance at the body

and shuddered. "I don't think I'll ever see this beach the same way again." Ellen and Dr. Soloski made their way back up the path.

Alva closed his box. He took the corn chips from Ruth's pocket and sprinkled them on the ground. Eleven birds came running to peck up the treat. "I'll help you get these critters home."

"I'll bring up the rear." Bobby gave Jack a smile. "Come by for a coffee refill when you get this mess under control."

King Kong couldn't prevent him from taking her up on that offer. "Thanks, Bobby, I will." He watched her small figure move up the path, her pace matched to Ruth's. Bobby reached out an arm and wrapped it around Ruth's shoulders. What he wouldn't give to have her arm wrapped around him. Nate's voice snapped him out of his reverie.

"Hey, boss?"

He returned to the grisly pile where his partner knelt. "What's up?"

Nate held back the neck of the man's wet suit with a pen. "What do you think about this?"

Jack squinted and then his eyes widened. "I think I should have been a dentist."

Ruth wasn't sure whether or not to report for filming on Monday morning. She spent the weekend reading about Indigo Orson. The past seemed much more attractive at the moment than remembering the awful present that included Reggie's untimely end. She grabbed her binder anyway and made her way to the plateau overlooking the sheltered cove. There was no one there. She sat on a card chair, snuggled farther into her jacket, and flipped through the pages.

> *A stranger life I could not imagine. Washed up on shore, all alone in an alien country was almost more than I could bear. I fancied I heard the words of my mother entreating me to keep going. Mama, who had taught me to read and write against the wishes of my father. Mama, who died from the same infection that killed him.*
>
> *They were gone. The Orsons, dead. I was completely alone. Yet in my terrible state, afloat on a plank of wood, He sent me a treasure. There it was, bobbing on the water, a small barrel, no bigger than a man's boot, but what it held would save me. I grabbed hold of it with all my strength and made for land. It was hard going, clawing against the waves which seemed determined to drag me out to sea.*
>
> *The sun beat down on my head though my*

fingers were numb with cold. The salt water stung
my eyes and the sight of those poor souls adrift in
the waves as I struggled through the water sickened
me. I could not hold on for a moment longer.
When I felt the gravel under my feet, my spirit was
renewed, and I fell to my knees praising Father in
heaven for deliverance. I was alive. I was alive.

The sound of a woman's voice startled Ruth. She looked up to find Ethan and Sandra, heads bent together, locked in intense conversation as they headed up the path toward the grassy clearing where she sat.

"But he's dead," Sandra said, choking back a sob. She turned her face toward the ocean below. "Reggie's dead."

Ethan held up a hand. "We couldn't have foreseen that. If he hadn't gone off on his own, this wouldn't have happened. You better believe he wouldn't hesitate to double-cross us."

"It doesn't matter what we did or didn't see coming. The man is dead. I. . ." Sandra jerked her head around as she caught sight of Ruth. "Oh, Mrs. Budge. I didn't think you would be here. I'm sure you've heard about. . .about Reggie."

"Yes. Alva and I found him on the beach, as a matter of fact. I'm very sorry."

"We are, too." Ethan's face was smooth, bare of emotion. "He was a great friend and colleague. It's a terrible tragedy."

A friend who would double-cross them about something? Ruth decided to indulge her nosiness. "Why was he diving at night?"

Ethan blinked. "At night? I don't know."

"Was he doing something for the film project?"

"No, definitely not. We would never have him do a night dive. That's much too dangerous."

Sandra tugged a strand of blond hair. "Maybe he was doing some recreational diving."

Ruth frowned. "That seems odd. What would he be able to see at night?"

"I'm sure the police will find out it was an accident. In any case, we're going to keep to the schedule as best we can. I'm going to see if I can get another cameraman out here, and if I can't, I'll take it over myself. Why don't you use the time today to read through the notebook and we'll start the filming as soon as possible. I'll let you know." Ethan turned his attention to an accordion file.

Sandra's mouth opened, but she didn't speak as Jack's police car pulled up the winding road.

Though Ruth would have liked nothing more than to eavesdrop on the conversation, she knew interfering in police business wasn't a good idea. Jack was a great friend, but first and foremost he was a cop. She waved good-bye and headed back to town to pick up the reluctant dental patient as promised.

Alva didn't answer when Ruth knocked. Finally Flo Hodges, who owned the small cottage where Alva rented a room, unlocked the door. Alva was under the bed.

Ruth peered into the dark space. "Please don't make me get down there, Alva. I'll be hard-pressed to get up again. Come on out. I'll take you over to Dr. Soloski's, and it will be over in no time. I promise."

"I don't wanna," came the plaintive voice.

"Tell you what. Why don't you come out, and I'll ask Bert Penny to give you a ride on his motorcycle after your tooth is fixed."

There was a moment of silence. "Really?"

"Really."

"Ya think he'd do it?"

"I'm sure he would if I asked him to."

There was movement from under the bed. "Well, all right then. I guess I can let the quack take a look."

"That's the spirit."

Ruth led the way as the two walked down the slope toward the town that squatted at the nostril end of Finny's Nose. Even with Alva's reluctant pace they arrived at the tidy office in less than twenty-five minutes. A nautical theme, right down to the rustic wood benches and abalone shell business-card holder, decorated the bright space. She had a mental picture of the dentist doing his work wearing a sailor's cap.

Dr. Soloski came out to greet them in the usual dentist garb. Alva hid behind Ruth.

"Good morning. How are you feeling, Ruth, after that awful thing on Saturday?"

"I'm all right, thanks. Trying not to think about it, mostly. I'm going to wait here for Alva, if that's okay." She stepped aside to reveal the cowering old man.

"Certainly. Come along, Mr. Hernandez." The doctor patted Alva on the shoulder. "We'll have you fixed up in no time."

Alva shot Ruth a desperate look as he was ushered into the back.

Ruth sighed. Her ankles felt puffy and swollen. How

was it possible that a fragile three-month-old fetus could wreak havoc on a perfectly serviceable body? That must be why people had babies in their twenties. With a twinge she remembered she'd had a baby then, too—her son, Bryce, who didn't want to be within spitting distance of her. Where had she gone wrong with him? And would she repeat the same mistakes with this late-in-life baby?

She shut down that depressing line of thought and turned her thoughts to Isabel Ortiz and her mysterious treasure. The page was still dog-eared where she'd left off reading that morning.

> *This is wild country. The men here are rough without the civilizing influence of women. The rush for gold has brought hundreds to this shore. They have eyes filled with desperation and want, a reckless need to throw every caution away in search of that elusive gold nugget. There are no women here and that is both a blessing and a curse.*
>
> *I decided from the earliest instance that I would be in great peril if these men found a helpless woman on their shore, a Mexican woman at that. They think anyone with skin of a different color is lower than a dog. When we were aboard the* Triton, *I heard tell of a group of white miners calling themselves "the hounds" that chased Mexican miners off their claims and beat them near to death. What could I do to save myself?*
>
> *It was then I became Indigo Orson. With my ragged, unkempt appearance, they had no reason to suspect my secret. A pair of grizzled old miners took*

*me in and let me sleep in a corner of their tent.
They were most curious about my barrel. I slept
with it under my head in the night.*

*With the first light of dawn, I opened my
treasure trove and prayed that God would give
me the courage to see it through. The barrel did
its work, and the flour was dry as dry could be. I
measured out a precious dip from inside. With a
borrowed pan and a bit of grease, I cooked up a
batch of biscuits, light as air and golden brown on
top. At the first smell of baking bread, the miners
emerged from their miserable hidey holes like
gophers from their burrows. They lined up around
my campfire to watch, mouths open, as I baked up
the biscuits. Imagine my surprise when one man
shouted, "I'll give ya five dollars for them biscuits."
Five dollars? Such a fortune for a bit of bread? To
these men who have been eating roots and berries
for months, the flour was treasure indeed.*

*I settled for one dollar per biscuit, and only
two per man. At the end of the morning I had a
ten-dollar gold piece and a handful of other coins.
God saved me with His white treasure. That night
with my pocket full of coins, I thanked Him and
said a prayer for Señor and Señora Orson, God rest
their souls.*

Ruth shook her head in amazement. Indigo Orson. A
Mexican woman, impersonating a man, cooking for half-
starved miners. She could imagine the fear that Indigo
felt, but that stubborn will to survive that could only come

from the Lord. The episode was better than fiction and certainly worthy of being documented on film. She hoped she would be able to do justice to the amazing lady.

With thoughts of Indigo swirling in her mind, Ruth dozed.

Less than an hour later, Alva stomped into the waiting room, shouting over his shoulder at the dentist, the plastic bib fluttering under his chin.

"You said it wasn't a-going to hurt. Whaddya call that needle poke, huh? A love pat?"

Dr. Soloski stiffened. "I guarantee you, Alva, no other dentist could have done a finer job on that tooth."

Alva's ears pinked as he continued his tirade. "How should I know what kinda job you did? Not like I could see yer work or anything. Maybe you left a tool in there or somethin'. Maybe I'm goin' to find a screwdriver in my mouth when I eat my snack today. Or maybe a chisel."

The dentist stared at him in openmouthed surprise. "There are no tools—"

Alva cut him off with a loud snort. "Never mind. It's all done and I'm still alive and kicking. Now where's my prize?"

Dr. Soloski's eyebrows furrowed. "Your prize?"

"Yeah. I talked to Ralphie over at the preschool and he says ya get a prize when yer finished at the dentist."

"Oh. Of course. I let the kids pick out a trinket. Help yourself." He pointed to a wooden chest filled with plastic toys and sugarless gum.

Alva turned to the reception desk and grabbed the

abalone shell. He carefully unloaded the business cards on the counter. "I'll take this."

"Alva," Ruth began, "he meant—"

Dr. Soloksi waved his hand. "It's okay, Mrs. Budge. I can find something else to hold my business cards. He's welcome to it if that will make him feel better about his appointment today."

Ruth guided Alva to the door. "You wait outside. I'll just be a minute."

When they were alone, she attempted an apology. "I'm so sorry, Dr. Soloski. Alva is just terrified of dentists, or doctors of any kind for that matter. You wouldn't believe what we had to do to get him in for a physical. The doctor gave up after an hour and pronounced him healthy."

The dentist ran a hand through his thick brown hair. "I know I shouldn't take offense. I'm a perfectionist. I see dentistry as an art as much as a science." He chuckled. "I've had people weep with joy at being relieved of their dental problems. I think Alva is a long way from that kind of response."

They both laughed. The phone rang. He sighed. "I'll just let the machine pick it up."

"Have you hired a receptionist yet?"

"No. I've had several applicants, but I'm a perfectionist in that area, too, I guess."

The door crashed open and Ellen Foots strode in, a plate of plastic-wrapped muffins in her hands. "Hello, Dr. Soloski." Her face tightened when she saw Ruth. "Oh, hello, Ruth." She turned her attention back to the dentist. "I was just in the neighborhood, and I thought I'd bring you some breakfast. I just whipped these up this morning."

Ruth peeked at the plump muffins. Blueberry, topped

with crumbs, and very familiar. They looked exactly like the kind sold at Monk's shop, a far cry from the hockey puck variety Ellen provided for the last library function. She watched the giantess smooth her frizzy hair.

Doctor Soloski patted his trim waist. "Oh. Why, thank you. I'll save them for later. Have to keep the body in shape and all."

"Of course. I'm a real fitness nut myself. I saw you out running one day, early. What time do you usually go?"

"Well, the time varies according to my schedule."

Ellen nodded. "Did you look over my application? I do have a dental health background, you know, and I could whip your schedule into shape in no time. If you don't take control of your schedule, it will take control of you, I always say."

Dr. Soloski's eyes widened a bit. Ruth gave him a sympathetic look and left the dentist with the formidable librarian.

Outside she found Alva stroking the pearlescent interior of the abalone. "It's a fine shell, ain't it?"

"Yes, Alva, but you weren't very polite to the dentist."

Alva blinked. "No?" His eyes narrowed with mischief. "I'll bet he'd rather have me in that there office than her." He pointed at Ellen Foots through the window. The woman seemed to have cornered the unfortunate dentist by the water cooler.

"I think you may be right about that."

~

She treated Alva to a chocolate milk, which he dribbled a bit due to his numb mouth, and herself to one of Al's black and white cookies. Thoroughly satiated with carbohydrates, she walked Alva home. It was close to one o'clock when she headed up the driveway to her small cottage. From the outside, it was impossible to detect the havoc Carson had created in his attempt to repair termite damage to an exterior wall. To the unsuspecting visitor, it was a cozy three-bedroom bungalow, surrounded by hydrangeas and a massive lemon tree.

She inhaled the delicate aroma of citrus as she approached the house. The scent always soothed her nerves. Before she could open the front door, an enormous man with close-cropped salt-and-pepper hair stepped out on the front step and wrapped her in a hug.

"Monk." Her eyes filled with tears. "I missed you. I feel like you've been gone forever."

He kissed the top of her head. "Me, too, baby. Me, too. Let me see you. How are you feeling? You look fantastic."

She laughed. "I've been told I look waxy and glazed. How is your father?"

"He's doing well. That stroke isn't going to slow him down for a minute. He's as determined as a freight train."

"Sounds like you came by your genes honestly."

"My mother is beside herself with excitement about this baby."

"I wish I could just be excited and leave all the other worries behind."

He rubbed her shoulders. "Don't you fret. We're going to work it out in good time. I'm just glad to be back home, with the crazy stuff that's going on here. Did they figure out what happened to that diver? I couldn't believe it when you called to tell me. The riptides must have gotten him."

"They're still investigating as far as I know. Let's go inside. I want to hear all about your trip."

He did a quick sidestep to prevent her from entering. "Well, honey, there's something I should tell you before you go in."

"Has Carson done something again? What else could he possibly have broken? We're already down one lamp and a picture frame. Is he aware that we're going to have to put a baby in that room in a matter of months?"

"No, no. It's not the house."

"It's not the house?" She took in his uneasy expression. "What's wrong, Monk?"

"Well, I wouldn't exactly say anything was wrong. It could be a real good thing, I mean, after you've got some time to think about it." He shifted his weight to the other foot.

"Monk."

"I know I should have called, and actually I tried, but you weren't home and I had to make a decision. I hope I did the right thing."

Her last shred of patience evaporated. "Monk, if you don't tell me what's going on right now I am going to start to howl at the top of my lungs."

Before he had time to answer, the door behind him opened.

Ruth's mouth fell open in shock.

5

Jack tightened the strap of his helmet. The bike wobbled as he pedaled, as if the wheels had a different direction in mind. After a few minutes he achieved the proper pedal to steer ratio and headed up slope, skirting the shadow of Finny's Nose.

This is ridiculous. I've got a murder to investigate. What am I doing on a bike right now?

In spite of his negative thoughts, he recognized the perfect beauty of the day. The Monday afternoon was warm, brilliant June sunshine broken by the thick canopy of eucalyptus and pine trees that bordered the trail. The scent of cedar mingled with the faint tang of the sea. Jack's cell phone chirped. He lurched to a stop and answered. He had to wait for Nate on the other end of the line to finish his sneezing fit. "God bless. When are you going to take some allergy medicine?"

"When they can make some that won't put me to sleep. You remember what happens when I fall asleep."

Jack smiled. Usually Nate's triplet girls attempted to paint his nails or use him as a Barbie dive platform when he slumbered at home. "What do you have from the lab?"

"Nothing yet," Nate said before he blew his nose. "And I'm still trying to find next of kin. Where are you? You sound winded."

"Uh, out. I'll be back in the office in a few hours."

Nate laughed. "Right. Tell Bobby I said hello."

Jack grunted and clicked off the phone just as Bobby

coasted up. Her cheeks were flushed pink from the combination of exertion and the temperature.

"Hi," he said, feeling his stomach do the two-step.

"Hi."

He fiddled with the handgrips and ran a finger under his chin strap. "So, uh, here we are."

"Yes, here we are." She sipped out of a water bottle.

"Nice day for a bike ride."

She wiped her mouth. "Yes, it is, but I have to admit I'm surprised, Jack."

"About what?"

"Lots of things. You're not in the office the Monday after a murder, for one thing."

"I went in early this morning, so I'm due to have a break. The bike riding idea was perfect." He took in her skeptical look. "I'm trying to find balance."

"Uh-huh. I didn't picture you as the bike-riding type."

He laughed. "Would you believe I'm a man of mystery?"

"No. Closemouthed, yes, but not really the mysterious type."

"Guilty as charged. I couldn't resist your invitation to go for a ride."

The wind picked up her black hair and tousled it across her eyes. "That's a surprise. Seems like you resist me plenty."

Jack stared at her, drinking in the pink of her cheeks, the wild sparkle in her dark eyes. Resist her? He couldn't get through one hour of the day without thinking about her, wondering where she was, wishing he could be there next to her. He tried to think of a safe way to put his feelings into words. Before he could answer, she stowed the bottle and pedaled off up the slope.

He gritted his teeth and followed.

The road was mostly gravel by the time they hit the top of Finny's Nose. Jack tried to control his gasping breaths as he dismounted and pressed a hand to the cramp in his side.

Bobby hiked past a cluster of manzanitas and sat on an outcropping of rock that provided an unobstructed view of the vast Pacific. A hummingbird zoomed in to check out the strange visitor to his territory, and she stayed still to put it at ease. The bird hovered for a moment, as if exchanging a greeting with her.

Jack watched her profile, the small nose, determined chin, short hair fluttering in the wind. For a moment, his breathing grew even more unsteady. He wanted to say so many things but found himself speechless.

"I always pictured California as having clear blue water and golden sand, until I came here." She regarded the gray waves that thundered onto the rocky beach below. He joined her, and they took in the gulls circling the beach in a great noisy cluster.

"I imagine that's what Frederick Finny was looking for when he wrecked his ship trying to smuggle rum along this coast. He was probably surprised about the beaches, too."

She giggled. "At least he got a mountain named after him."

"More of a big hill really."

Jack's eyes narrowed at the sight of a stranger picking his way along the sand. The man was tall, his gait purposeful. Jack wished they were closer so he could make out the face. Strangers were uncommon on this rough bit of coastline. Visitors tended to gravitate toward

Honey Beach or the quaint shops and restaurants in town. Many made a beeline for Roxie Trotter and her fishing excursions.

And some visitors wound up murdered on Finny's unforgiving shore, he reminded himself. The cameraman was actually the third murder since last October.

Bobby handed him a thermos of coffee. Her fingers seemed to generate their own heat where they touched his hand.

"You brought coffee? How did you know I'd be ready for some?"

She smiled. "Because I've never known you not to be in the mood for some java."

He took a hefty slug of the brew, burning his tongue in the process. "When is Monk coming back?"

"He flew in this morning. Apparently he ran into Ruth's son at the airport."

"Bryce?"

She nodded. "Bryce is going to stay with them, I think."

Jack wondered how that would go over with the man's newly pregnant mother. Then his mind raced ahead to the implications of Monk's return. "But you're going to stay for a while? That's what you said, right?"

"Maybe until Ruth's baby comes. Or until I get a job offer. I'm not sure."

He watched the soft curve of her lip, so prone to break into a smile. It brought him back to another face, a face from his other life. The two faces were so alike, and so different.

Bobby fixed her black eyes on his. "What are you thinking about?"

"Me? Nothing."

Her brows knitted. "Here's an idea. How about you tell me the truth? Even if it's personal or you think it makes you look silly."

There was no anger in her words but a trace of sadness that he wanted to erase. He tried to breathe out the weight that settled in his chest. "I was thinking about Lacey."

"You miss her."

"Yes. She's been dead for more than two years, but it doesn't feel like that sometimes." It seemed like only a moment ago when he'd gotten the call. Lacey dead from a brain hemorrhage at the foot of their driveway, with their toddler son, Paul, watching it all from the window. Was it only a few years ago? Or a lifetime?

The stranger Jack had noticed before now disappeared around a rugged cliff. Jack cleared his throat. "She was always asking me to take time away from work. To go on picnics or bike rides, especially after Paul was born. She was a big one for taking nature walks."

Bobby's voice was low. "And you didn't go very often?"

"Not enough."

"She sounds like a very smart woman."

"She was. She had a lot of heart, like you do." He looked down at his scuffed shoes.

"Jack, do you feel guilty for having feelings for me?"

He swallowed. Hard. He wanted to deny it. Instead the words came out haltingly, like a deer trying to stand on newborn legs. "I. . .yes."

For a moment she was expressionless. Then her face lit with a smile. She leaned toward him and pressed her lips against his, soft and gentle. "Thank you for being honest.

I guess you really do care about me."

When his breath returned, he wanted to crush her to him, to bury his face in her neck and shut out the world, and his guilt. Instead he whispered a prayer. "God help me."

Bobby gave him that sideways tilt of her head. "He is, Jack. He's helping you heal."

"How do you figure?"

"It's like being in the ocean and swimming back to shore. You've got to go through the rough surf sometimes, but it has to be done, no matter how uncomfortable. Otherwise, you're just—"

"Treading water?"

Her eyes sparkled. "Exactly, and sooner or later that doesn't work anymore."

His phone rang again. With clumsy fingers he answered, listening intently. "I'm on my way."

"I hope it's not another body."

"No, not this time, but I do have to get going."

Bobby laughed and checked her watch. "Well, that was one hour and forty-three minutes away from work. Not bad."

He sighed as they retrieved their bikes. "It's a start, anyway."

The station was in the usual state of chaos when he returned. Alva lay on his back on the front counter. His heavy black boots overlapped one side of the Formica, and his knit cap jutted over the other, a tiny blue pom-pom clearly visible. "I wanna report a theft. I got my rights to report a crime, ain't I? Look in here, just look why don'tcha?"

Jack tried to sneak past into his office, but he couldn't get by the angry lady in front of him.

Maude Stone stiffened her minuscule frame. "You are an idiot, Alva Hernandez. A moron of the highest degree. Why do you even pay attention to him, Mary?"

Officer Mary Dirisi reached over Alva's stomach for a pen. "Because he's lying on my workspace. Okay, Alva, I've got a report to do, so spill it. What's the deal?"

Alva shoved a finger into his mouth and angled his face in the officer's direction. "Aarrrgh uz iitttte ere."

"What?" she said, pencil poised.

"Arrggh us ittt—"

Jack squelched a smile.

"You imbecile, take your finger out of your mouth!" Maude yelled so loud it echoed through the office.

Alva removed his finger. "That quack dentist stole my tooth. I had one way in the back and now it's gone. I didn't notice until the Novocain wore off. He stole it, sure as shootin'. That's grand theft dentistry. He probably sells 'em on the black market to toothless people in Bangladesh."

"I don't think people even in Bangladesh are that desperate for teeth," Mary said, scribbling on a form.

Alva considered this. "Well, maybe he took 'em for some other reason. Could be he sells 'em as fake relics to churches. Now my tooth might be from St. Alva, Patron Saint of Molars."

Maude snorted. "Patron Saint of Fools is more like it. Alva, shut up and listen. Dr. Soloski probably explained everything to you, but you were too ding blasted stubborn to pay attention. I spoke to him earlier, and he told me that when he was putting in your filling, he noticed you had a chipped molar and he filed it. It's not gone, you nitwit, it's probably just smoothed down so it feels different."

The old man sat up. His eyebrows undulated as he explored the area with his tongue. Mary handed him a mirror from her purse.

He peered into his mouth, moving his head this way and that to get a better view. "Well, I'll be a smitten toad. There it is. I guess he ain't stoled my tooth. How about that?"

"No," Maude said, "but somebody stole your brain. Now quit maligning Dr. Soloksi. We need all the professional men we can get in this town."

Maude caught sight of Jack edging toward his office. "Oh, there you are, Detective. I've been trying to find you since Saturday. I want to know what's going on with this murder investigation. What exactly is the status? Do you have any suspects? Made any arrests? It's terrible for our Finny image. What will people say?"

Probably the same thing they said after the murder at the Finny Fog Festival in March, he thought. "Don't worry, Maude. People will still flock to Finny for the clean air and great fishing. Nothing will tarnish our quaint fishing village appeal."

Maude opened her mouth, but Jack cut her off. "I've got a meeting. Talk to Officer Dirisi if you have any more specific questions."

Mary shot him a poisonous look as he escaped into his office.

He eased into his chair and took the cup of coffee Nate handed him, feeling only a twinge of guilt at leaving

Mary at Maude's mercy.

Nate blew his nose. "How's Bobby?"

"She's fine." He ignored the sly smile under Nate's bushy mustache. "What's the word?"

"Well, we notified next of kin, a mother in Des Moines. We got the sheets back on him and it seems as though Reggie was into some trouble, small stuff mostly. Petty theft, fencing stolen merchandise, anything to earn a quick buck."

"Funding a drug habit?"

"Nah, gambling debts."

"Okay, the guy needed quick cash." Jack tapped a pencil on the desk. "How does that put him in the ocean at night?"

"Could be unrelated. Maybe he dove for fun. He was into all that survival stuff."

Jack eyed the crease in Nate's forehead. "But you don't think so?"

"No. What are you going to see diving at night in those rough waters? Even Jacques Cousteau couldn't handle that in his little submarine thingy. And Reggie didn't have a camera that we can find anyway, just a real nice underwater flashlight and some light sticks. The guys from county also found his line with a full tank attached."

"Full?" Jack's mind raced. "He set up an extra tank, planning on doing some deep diving, but he never got the chance. Is this about that shipwreck?"

"Don't know. The college people insisted they are interested in it purely as a research project. Last group that dove the wreck years ago didn't find much of anything anyway. 'Course we had that killer storm awhile back.

Maybe that stirred something up."

"Let's get Sandra and Ethan in here and apply some pressure."

"They'll be here at three o'clock."

"Okay."

Jack felt a vein pound behind his left eye along with tightness in his quads from the bike ride. "Pictures?"

Nate slid a set of digital photos over the desk and pointed. "No official word from the coroner yet, but I'm thinking this little baby did him in, not the ocean."

Jack squinted at the rope wrapped around the victim's neck in the picture. "I've never seen a knot like that."

"Me neither. Looks like some kind of sailor's knot. I wonder if Monk knows it. He's an old sea dog."

"I'll head over there later."

Mary poked her head into the office. "I got rid of Maude but only after promising someone will give her a call later today. That someone is not going to be me."

Jack sighed. "I don't get paid enough to endure Maude Stone."

Mary flipped her braid over her shoulder. "None of us do, but I just did my turn, remember? Coroner's office called. You were right, Nate. Guy was strangled."

Nate thumped his chest. "I am Ubercop, ruler of the police world. I am invincible."

Jack laughed. "Well, Ubercop, give my regards to Maude when you call her this afternoon."

6

*T*he men are dirty. Rough and coarse, with long matted hair and hands hardened into claws. They treat me well, though, because I am the only one who can cook. Even so, I daren't tell them I'm a woman or all would be lost. It is a dangerous place here for all but intolerable for the female species. I heard tell that the vaqueros ride among the Indian villages and drive out the young girls and sell them for 100 dollars each. How can it be true? With such tales, I have no choice but to remain Indigo Orson.

The day I went to town for supplies, I came upon a group of men standing next to their long tom, watching a pot on the fire, looking as if they had been knocked down. Come to be known, they were trying to figure out why their rice was not cooked properly. I told them in as gruff a way as I could manage, to add water to the pot! Imagine. They are without even the most basic skills. Probably they never gave a thought to how their women back home prepared the meals or mended the clothes. What they would give for their wives' home-cooked specialties or excellent laundering now. They say men are the stronger species, but here they have been reduced to little children without the civilizing influence of women.

Children. Now there was a touchy subject. Ruth closed the binder and sipped from her thermos of hot tea. The Tuesday morning sun was barely approaching the horizon and her cheeks were cold. She'd left Monk snoring softly and tiptoed away down to the beach. Now her thoughts rolled like the waves that heaved along with her stomach.

Bryce was back.

The son she hadn't seen since her first husband's funeral greeted her with a "Hi, Mom," as he emerged from around Monk's back.

Hi, Mom, as if he was stopping in for his daily visit.

It would be more natural if he called her Ruth. That would fit the distant relationship they endured. He was twenty-six now, but he looked older. And different somehow. Ruth pulled her hood tighter as she remembered. He looked a trifle. . .uncertain. She did not recall seeing anything but a confident look on his face the last few times she'd encountered him.

Monk appeared and lowered his bulky frame onto the rock next to her. The shadows under his eyes marked a fitful sleep. "All right, let's get it out on the table. How much trouble am I in exactly? I'm here to take my medicine."

"No trouble. It took me by surprise, that's all." Surprise? More like total shock. They'd managed a few forced pleasantries before Bryce retreated to the guest room and her to the bathtub.

Monk sighed. "Honestly, he surprised the stuffing out of me, too. There I am, just getting off the plane at the San Francisco airport and this young fella comes up to me and says he thinks we know each other. I didn't even recognize him, but he whipped out our wedding picture.

Doggone if the guy isn't your son. Imagine my surprise to find out he was on his way here. What are the odds of that happening at an international airport?"

Bryce carried around their wedding picture? She swallowed some now tepid chamomile, supposedly a cure for morning sickness. It left her watery and every bit as nauseated. "So you invited him to stay with us."

"Uh, well, yes." Monk pushed a pile of sand around with his shoe. "It didn't seem right sending him to the Finny Hotel, him being your son and all. I tried to call you, honey, really. I didn't want to spring it on you out of the blue."

She looked at the crinkles around his eyes. No, he couldn't have sent her son to the hotel. His big heart wouldn't have allowed that. It was clear how much agony the decision inflicted on him. She squeezed his hand. "You did the right thing, and I'm not mad about it. But why did Bryce come here, Monk? Now, I mean. He didn't even come for our wedding." His absence hurt her more than she could put into words.

"He didn't say, but I got the feeling he's had some trouble."

"What kind of trouble?"

"I don't know exactly. I expect he'll get around to telling you."

She wasn't so sure. The waves left ribbons of foam on the beach. Further down, an area of sand was blocked off with yellow tape. She shuddered and turned her eyes away.

A crunch of gravel made them both turn. Dr. Soloski, dressed in sweats, huffed up the trail. When he saw them he turned off his iPod and slowed to jog in place. "Morning again. How's Mr. Hernandez holding up?"

"Alva's fine, Dr. Soloski," Ruth said. *Once he figured out you didn't steal his tooth and send it to Bangladesh,* she thought with a smile. "I've never seen you take this path before."

He shot an uneasy look over his shoulder. "Oh, well, I thought I'd check out the view. I can't get enough of coastal living."

Monk chuckled. "You're a sucker for the fresh sea air?"

"You bet. Cities aren't for the likes of me. I avoid them like the plague." His eyebrows creased. "Did you hear something?"

They listened for a moment until they heard the sound of approaching feet.

The dentist turned on his music and waved. "I'm off then. Talk to you soon." He sprinted away.

"He's in an awful hurry," Monk said.

Five seconds later Ellen Foots careened down the trail. Her mane of hair was twisted into two stiff black ropes that protruded from the top of her scalp like the knobs on a giraffe's head. She was dressed from neck to ankle in shiny green spandex.

She pounded to a stop and looked around. "Where is he?"

"Who?" Ruth said.

"Dr. Soloski."

Monk beamed. "Why? Did you have a dental emergency, Ellen?"

"Of course not. My teeth are in excellent condition. I use an ultrasonic cleaner and fluoride rinse every day. I just happened to be out for a jog, and I thought I saw Dr. Soloski."

Through binoculars from her perch in the top of a tree, Ruth thought. "I didn't know you were a runner."

She shuffled a bit, the gravel crunching under her sneakers. "I decided to take it up. A person can never be too healthy. The body is the temple, after all." A flicker of movement in the distance caught her eye. "There he is."

Ellen darted off.

"I hope he runs fast. He's gonna need to break some sprinting records to outrun her." Monk helped Ruth to her feet. "Home again, my love?"

"Uh, no, er, I think I have a rehearsal."

His thick eyebrow lifted. "Really? In view of the murder, I didn't think there was anything to rehearse."

"I promised I'd check in again, anyway. Sandra and Ethan are meeting me at the hotel."

"I'll go with you."

"That's okay. You go on home and see if. . .if Bryce needs anything."

He wrapped her in a final hug. "I love you, Ruthy. It's going to be okay. You'll see."

She could feel his gaze as she headed toward the center of town.

Sandra and Ethan sat in the lobby of the Finny Hotel, papers strewn on the oak table. The place was dark, a sharp contrast to the vibrant bougainvillea that painted the outside of the building with fluorescent orange and pink. Ruth took a deep breath to settle her stomach. "Good morning. I thought I'd come by and check on the schedule."

Sandra looked up from her clipboard. "Oh, hi, Ruth. Um, I really appreciate you coming all the way here but, you know, I don't think we're going to rehearse today. We've got some work to do."

Ethan pushed the wire rim glasses up his nose. "Sandy and I need to retool a bit. We've only got a week left to wrap this up before the next term starts, so we'll start filming tomorrow maybe."

"Will that give you enough time to finish?"

Sandra blinked. "Finish? Oh sure, sure."

"Who is going to run the camera?"

"I will," Ethan said. "I'm not as good as Reggie but I get by. It's too much to find another guy at this point."

Ruth thought back to Indigo's scrawled passages. "I read that the *Triton* has been excavated before. Did they find anything interesting?"

Sandra gave her a sharp look. "Interesting? Not really. It was a coal transport so there wasn't much to find. Why?"

"I just wondered."

Ethan's eyes narrowed. "There's nothing on that boat but coal. Whatever artifacts there were have long since been removed or covered with barnacles."

Ruth wondered at his strong tone. "Are you going to take any more underwater footage? It seems so dangerous."

Ethan shook his head. "No, we're not filming anything else in the ocean. We'll work around it. Sandy will let you know when we're going to rehearse again." He turned back to the open laptop.

Sandra wiggled her fingers in a good-bye.

Ruth met Alva as she exited the hotel. "Howdy, sweet cheeks. Time for a snack. Want some candy?"

She took the can opener from him and then the dentist's shell while he searched his pockets and produced a bag of candy.

"Here you go. Did I tell you old Alva would take care of you? Say, I checked the beach this morning but there wasn't no more bodies." He looked disappointed as he rooted around in his pockets, emerging with another small bag.

"Thanks, Alva. You really are a gift from God." She admired the play of afternoon sunshine on the pearlescent interior of the shell as she handed it back along with the can opener. "Don't you think you should give this back to Dr. Soloski?"

"Why? He didn't have nothing to do with finding that can opener."

"Not the can opener, the shell."

"Give it back? Huh-uh. He told me to pick a prize. That there's mine now." He shoveled in a handful of candy corns. "Where are you headed?"

She sighed. "Back home, I guess. My son is here."

He looked with wild eyes from her head to her stomach. "What? How'd it get out that quick? How come you're still inflated?"

"No, no. Not this baby. My son, Bryce. He's a grown man now. You probably met him when he lived here a long time ago."

Alva screwed up his face. "Bryce, Bryce. Oh yeah. Serious little guy? Always playing by himself?"

Ruth cringed. "Yes, that's him."

"Does he still like to dig at the beach?"

She had a sudden memory of Bryce as a little boy,

holding a small plastic pail and shovel, solemnly scooping out holes in the sand. "I don't know what he likes anymore, Alva. I guess it's time for me to go find out."

Ruth tiptoed into the quiet house. Her husband was gone, she knew, busy at Monk's Coffee and Catering. She listened for sounds of movement. Nothing but the tick of the grandfather clock. With a sigh of relief, she headed into the kitchen in search of orange juice.

Bryce sat at the table, reading the paper. He looked up with eyes that reminded her so much of Phillip's.

Her breath caught for a moment, heart pounding in her chest. "Hello, Bryce."

He nodded. "Morning. Not much news here in Finny, is there?"

"Not as much as Chicago, I imagine."

"There is an article about the man you found on the beach. It says the cause of death is under investigation. Is Jack handling the case?"

She nodded.

"I figured it was a diving accident. Those are rough waters, easy to lose your bearings."

"Yes. I sure wouldn't want to dive there." The kitchen melted into silence. "Um, do you want me to fix you some lunch?" It brought her back a couple of decades, when she was a doting mother, trying to do anything and everything for a spoiled little boy.

"No thanks. I'm not hungry. I made myself some coffee. Hope that was okay." He folded the newspaper into a precise rectangle.

She wasn't sure whether to sit at the table or take her juice to the other room. She settled for standing and sipping.

He looked at her, his face an unreadable mask. "I didn't know you were expecting."

Her face heated. "Oh, yes, I meant to tell you, but I just never managed to make the call. Things have been really crazy here." The excuse sounded lame to her own ears.

"When are you due?"

"December."

"Oh." He drummed his fingers on the table. "A baby, wow. That's unusual for someone. . .in your phase of life."

She flushed. At least he hadn't said *old*. "It is, but we're both happy about it." *Happy and terrified beyond all reason.*

"Roslyn was pregnant, too."

The words startled her, as did the flood of emotion that they caused. "Bryce, that's—" Her flutter of excitement was fleeting. "Was?"

"She lost the baby at three months."

Ruth's heart twisted at the tremor in his voice. "I'm so sorry."

He shrugged. "The doctor says it happens and most of the time they never know the reason." He shook his head as if to clear the memory away. "Monk says you're doing all right. I guess that means I'm going to have a brother or sister."

"One or the other. We didn't want to know ahead." She gulped some juice. "Um, how do you, uh, feel about that?"

"I'm not sure. It doesn't really matter how I feel about it anyway, does it?"

She was not sure what to say in response so she settled

on a change in topic. "So, what brings you to Finny?"

"Roslyn."

"Are you vacationing here together?"

"No. She left me."

Ruth coughed. "Roslyn left?"

"Yeah. She met someone. A florist, if you can call him that." He spat out the words. "The guy sells flowers out of a roadside shack. He rides a moped to work."

Her breath caught at the anger that was written in his clenched jaw and the deep crease in his forehead.

Bryce sat ramrod straight in the chair. "The business failed, too."

The business, too? Bryce had taken on his wife's family trucking company when they married. From the rare Christmas card, she gathered it had been doing well. Until now.

There was something about his face, a streak of small child vulnerability mixed in with the anger, that gave her the sudden urge to wrap her grown boy in a hug. She knew it would not do, just as it had not satisfied him twenty years ago. She could not fix this problem for him and he wouldn't want her to try.

Instead, she laid a hand lightly on his arm. "I'm so sorry, Bryce, about everything, especially the baby."

He did not look at her.

He did not move away.

"Yeah," he said, his voice awash in bitterness. "Me, too."

The sun mellowed its way into the hills. From her seat in the luscious pool of sunlight next to the worm beds, Ruth offered up a prayer of thanks. "Thank You, Lord, for this precious day. Thank You for letting this baby inside me have another day to grow and flourish. Please reach out Your healing hands to Bryce and help me to give him what he needs right now."

She hadn't finished the amen when Monk opened the sliding door and ushered Roxie into the backyard. The woman blinked and rubbed under her nose with a red handkerchief. "I came for my worms. I've got a couple booked for a fishing expedition tomorrow, and I promised to provide the bait."

"That's great." Ruth searched through the white plastic tubs for Roxie's. "How's business?"

She shrugged. "Not great. I've had a few folks book for this week and next, but it would be better if those collegiate types would leave."

Ruth found the container and handed it to Roxie. "Are they causing problems for you?"

"Nothing terrible. It just makes me nervous, them slipping in and out of the water. My customers like to think they're the only people allowed in the ocean at any given time. The happier they are, the better my business."

Ruth perked up. "You've seen Sandy and Ethan diving? When?"

"Last two nights, just after sundown."

After sundown? "Were they taking pictures, do you think?"

"I didn't see a camera, only flashlights. They're up to something. No one should be in the water late. That's insanity. They didn't learn a thing from their cameraman dying in those waters. People can be so stupid, especially when they're young."

The door opened again, and Bryce stuck his head out. "Monk said to tell you dinner's ready." He shot Roxie a curious look. "Hello."

Roxie waved a hand at him.

"Thanks, Bryce. I'll just be a minute." Ruth finished packaging up the worms.

"Who was that?"

"My son."

"I didn't know you had kids."

"He's visiting from Chicago."

"Crazy city." Roxie looked back at the door, an odd expression on her face.

"Do you have children, Roxie?"

"Me? No." Ruth almost didn't hear the second whispered comment. "Not anymore."

Ruth watched her pull at a hole in her knit cap. "Would you like to join us for dinner? Monk's making his famous meatballs, and there's always enough for an army. We'd love to have you."

"No. Thanks for the offer, but I've probably overstayed my welcome already. I'll take my worms and get out of your hair."

Ruth led her back through the cottage to the front door, watching until the woman was out of sight. She stood there for a moment, breathing in the evening air that had turned cool and the savory smells of oregano and browning meat from the kitchen.

So the college students were hiding something, busy making night dives in spite of their comments to the contrary. Roxie was right. No one should be in the water that late.

Then again, why was Roxie?

7

"I'm mighty glad to have my niece home." Monk slid Jack a heavy mug filled with coffee. There was a lull in the Wednesday morning breakfast traffic so he untied his apron.

"Me, too. Bobby seems like she belongs in Finny." They walked to a table by the window. Jack tried to look casual as he looked around the coffee counter. "Is she here today?"

"She's visiting Ruth, but she'll be along later." He eyed the detective. "If you dillydally with that coffee long enough, you'll see her."

Jack felt his cheeks warm. He cleared his throat. "I actually came to see you. Official police business." He pushed a photograph toward the big man. "What do you make of this?"

Monk squinted at the paper. "Is this the knot tied around his—"

"Uh-huh."

"I've used many a knot in my day, but I've never seen one used like that on a person. I thought the man drowned."

"No. Coroner says he was strangled and then dumped in the water. I wondered if you could tell me anything about the knot."

Monk scratched his stubbled head and looked again. "It's a figure eight on a bight. Not too fancy, easy to do with some practice. I imagine plenty of folks use them but me; it's not my favorite."

"How so?"

"It would be difficult to untie after you had a heavy load on it, which is why the murderer didn't take the time to remove it, I'd imagine. Plus it's bulky, and it takes a lot of rope to make."

Jack sighed. "So you can't deduce that this knot was tied by a left-handed ex-sailor with brown eyes and a size 14 shoe?"

Monk drained his cup. "Sorry, no. I'm no Hercule Poirot. Ruth's the mystery solver in our family. I guess I didn't solve your case for you then."

"Afraid not but it was worth a try. How is Ruth getting on these days?"

Monk grinned sheepishly. "Fine as can be. 'Course having her grown son sprung on her was kind of a shock, especially after finding a body and all."

"Is Bryce staying with you two?"

"Uh-huh. One big happy family." He sipped some coffee. "Not that it's my business or anything, but Bobby and I were jawing last night and she says she might take a job out of state. Seems pretty serious about it, too, Jack."

Jack nodded, swallowing the odd feeling of panic that rose in his gut.

Monk raised an eyebrow. "I'd sure hate to see her leave, a great girl like that. Wouldn't you?"

Jack busied himself gulping coffee to avoid an answer.

A couple came in with cameras around their necks, cheeks flushed. "Excuse me," Monk said. "They look like they need some reviving."

"Don't we all," Jack muttered as he left the shop.

He opened the door and stepped through, just in

time to stumble into Bobby, almost knocking her down the front step. He reached out and caught her, and his heart kicked into overdrive. "Good morning."

She regained her footing. "Good morning. Did you come for your coffee fix?"

"Yes, ma'am. How is Ruth feeling?"

"Sick, but otherwise okay." She eyed him closely. "How are you? You look tired."

He chuckled. "I think that's the look you get when you pin on a police badge. It's a perpetual part of the uniform."

She laughed. "Can I come over and play with Paul after I pick up Uncle Monk's supplies this afternoon? I bought him some more Legos so that we can make a pirate ship. It's really cool."

"You bet." He tried to sound casual, but his pulse began to pound at the prospect of sharing an evening with her. "Um. . .when. . .around what time will you come around?"

"I'm thinking four-ish. Louella will let me in, won't she?"

"Of course. She'll be thrilled. I'll call her and give her the heads-up."

"Don't do that. She'll start cooking up a storm."

"Yes, but you always put her in a panic, being a vegetarian and all. She's convinced if you tasted her pot roast, you'd become a meat eater on the spot."

Their laughter mingled as Bobby walked around him into the shop. "See you later, gator."

He inhaled the scent of strawberry shampoo as he jogged back to his car, with a new energy that had nothing to do with caffeine.

Sandra Marconi shifted in her chair in the conference room. "Are we almost done?"

Jack nodded. "Pretty much, but I want to know why you're here, and I don't think you've quite given me that yet."

She blinked, eyes wide above her full cheeks. "Why we're here? I thought I explained all that. It's a project for our thesis. Ethan and I are filming a documentary about the—"

"The wreck of the *Triton*, I know. You told me that before. But according to your college neither of you are enrolled at the moment."

"Oh, that. We had to take a semester off, is all."

"Why?"

Her gaze darted back and forth before returning to Jack's face. "Because we couldn't keep up with a full load of classes and still get this project done, among other things."

"What other things?"

"Money things. College isn't cheap, you know."

"So you had to drop for a term. Why not wait on the project?"

"The timing is right to do it now. It's the anniversary and—"

"Isn't it unusual for college sophomores to take on such a big project? Why wouldn't you want to wait until your senior year maybe?"

She straightened. "Sometimes you've just got to move on a gut feeling, you know?"

The words vibrated in his ears. "I understand that."

"But you still think I'm hiding something?"

"I've been a cop for a long time, Ms. Marconi. I've learned that when something strikes me as odd, it bears checking into. I find it odd, that's all. Risky, to leave school. Why not film later in the summer during break?"

"Then we'd be here along with the other tourists."

"That's not usually too much of a problem in Finny."

"If we can pull off this project, the university will be impressed, maybe even impressed enough to offer us a scholarship."

"Sounds pretty iffy."

She sighed. "I suppose it is. Call us optimists, I guess."

His stomach grumbled to remind him he'd skipped breakfast again. "Who's bankrolling the project then if it isn't the college?"

"We got a five-thousand-dollar grant."

"From whom?"

She picked at a thread on her shorts. "I'm not sure it's public information."

He waited a beat. "There's no such thing as private information during a murder investigation. Who is bankrolling you?"

"The Skylar Foundation."

"Tell me about them."

"I don't really know anything about them. You'll have to ask Ethan."

He made a note on his pad. "One more thing. How are you going to finish your project without a photographer?"

"Ethan's going to film it."

He saw a flicker of uncertainty in her blue eyes.

"Ethan? He's got quite a few talents. Okay. That'll do for a while. You're free to go."

When the door closed behind her he called to Nate, who was trying to unclog his pencil sharpener. "Ever heard of the Skylar Foundation?"

"Nope."

"They give grants to students."

"Do they provide financial assistance to precocious six-year-old triplets?"

"I don't know, but you can ask them when you call."

———

He made it back home a few minutes to four, in time to kiss Louella and usher her to the door.

"Why the rush, Jack?" She put her hands on her massive hips. "Don't you tell me. You're having a lady over." Her round face crinkled in alarm. "My stars, you didn't tell me again. I should have cooked. I could have whipped up a nice lasagna. There's hardly any meat in that. I can fix you some chicken. Does a chicken count as meat?" Her eyes rolled in thought. "They're mostly bones and beak."

He helped her pull on a sweater, ignoring the grin that expanded her face a few more inches. "No need to cook anything. I just thought I'd come home early."

Her eyebrow arched in disbelief.

"And Bobby might come by," he admitted.

She kissed Paul good-bye. "Well, if you ask me, it's about time. I saw Bobby chatting with a handsome young man yesterday. Fine girl like that won't wait around forever."

The word shot out like a cannonball. "Who?"

"Don't know," Louella said, gathering her purse. She leveled a serious look at him. "But maybe you ought to find out, Mr. Detective."

The door closed behind her and Paul peeked out around the corner, a chocolate milk mustache dark on his pale skin. "Scary Bear?"

For the hundredth time, Jack thanked God for letting Paul talk again. The period of selective mutism the boy suffered after watching Lacey die nearly put him over the edge. Every word, every syllable was precious now.

"You'd better run, little man. Big Scary Bear is coming." With a growl he took off running after the happily shrieking boy. He caught Paul on the back porch, throwing him over his shoulder and doing his loudest bear impression. "Now Big Scary Bear is going to eat you for dinner."

Paul hollered and laughed as Jack tickled him.

They both stopped short to see Bobby come through the side gate. She stooped to pet Mr. Boo Boo, who promptly rolled over to give her access to his canine belly.

"Hi," she said. "I knocked but no one answered. I heard a bear on the rampage, so I let myself in the backyard. Hope that's okay." Her black eyes sparkled.

His stomach fluttered. "You bet. Sure. No problem."

"Hey, Paul." Bobby held up a Lego box and shook it. "I got some new ones so we can make that pirate ship."

"Daddy, down."

Jack righted the boy, who took off like an arrow toward Bobby, pulling her inside. "Let's go make our ship."

"Right, Captain Paul, but I get to be first mate." She laughed as Paul tugged her toward his room.

"Can you stay for dinner?" Jack called to her back.

"If it's no trouble," she said as she vanished down the hall.
"No trouble!"

He pumped his fist in a silent victory cheer and went to unpack the groceries he'd picked up on the way home. As he laid out the food, Louella's words intruded on his happiness. Bobby had been talking with a handsome man? Someone Louella didn't know? Must be an outsider. It wouldn't be hard to find out and he was going to. Soon.

He put the thought aside and went to work warming cheese quiche and slicing green beans to steam. Strawberries and melon and a side of hot dog for Paul. The hot dog made his mouth water, but he wasn't about to give in to his carnivorous instincts in front of vegetarian Bobby. *Best behavior, Jack.*

When he finally finished the dinner preparations, he went to find them. They weren't in Paul's room. Following the sound of laughter, he found them in the studio. For one second, he couldn't breathe.

It was a room he hadn't entered since the day he had buried his wife, a room that still smelled of her paints, though the tubes had long since dried out. Paul sat on Bobby's shoulders, pointing to an amateurish oil painting of a sunrise.

Jack had never understood Lacey's desire to paint, hours spent with brushes and palettes to produce a painting that would never be sold, or most likely even hung up. "What's the point?" he asked, after a particularly bad day at the office.

She looked at him, blond hair pulled back and green eyes much older than her twenty-eight years. "Because you never know when there's something beautiful right at your fingertips."

He'd been too much of a fool to see the beautiful thing he had until it was too late.

Bobby looked up. "Nice paintings. I'm a wreck at art. I can't even draw a stick man. Best I can do is a smiley face and even that turns out looking like a football most of the time."

He opened his mouth, but nothing came out.

She looked closely at his face and then lifted Paul down. He scampered down the hallway. "Um, I think maybe I wasn't supposed to come in here. I'm sorry. I should have asked first. I didn't realize it would upset you."

He managed a wan smile. "No, nothing like that. I, er, don't come in here much."

She slowly wrapped him in a tight hug. He burrowed his face into her neck, soaking in the satiny feeling of her skin. After a long moment he took her hand and led her out, carefully closing the door behind them.

"Paul said his mommy loved to paint."

Jack blinked some tears away. "Did he? He doesn't talk much about his mom. I wasn't sure he remembered that."

"I'm glad he does."

"Me, too." Jack held her hand as they returned to the kitchen.

Paul and Bobby hauled out the Lego creation they'd built and put it on the table. It made a fine centerpiece.

Jack raised his glass of tea. "To a couple of excellent construction workers and very accomplished pirates."

"Arrrgggh," Bobby said in reply.

They clinked glasses and dug in.

Paul looked pleased, Jack thought, as he wolfed down his hot dog. When he trotted off to find more Legos, Bobby chuckled. "He's talking quite a bit more now than he did when I first met him. Long sentences and everything. You must be happy."

"Beyond happy, I'd say. He still goes quiet when he's upset, and that gets my heart thumping, but so far we're weathering the storms pretty well. I. . .uh. . .notice he always seems to be extra chatty when you're around." His cell phone rang. He excused himself and answered, taking a few steps into the front room.

Nate gave him the report. "Cagey bunch, the Skylars. I've had to beat the phone bushes and cyber pavement to get anything on them."

"And what did you find on the elusive Skylar Foundation?"

"It's not much of a foundation. More like a salvage company, funded by a guy named Barnaby Skylar. He likes to provide the odd grant to folks involved in historical research."

"Well, that fits."

"Yeah."

Jack picked up the hesitation in Nate's voice. "So what's eating you?"

"There's very little info on his past projects. He's not affiliated with the university, I can tell you that much."

"So you don't think he's bankrolling Sandra and Ethan out of the goodness of his heart, or to get credit in their paper?"

"Not likely."

"Okay, Nate. Keep on it."

He hung up.

"Did I hear you say the Sklyar Foundation?" Bobby pushed her plate away as he joined her again.

"Yeah. It's the group that supposedly funded the film crew that's poking around here. You ever heard of it?"

"Yes." She frowned, twisting a strand of her straight black hair. "But I can't remember where. It will come to me. Of course, you could just ask Ethan."

Jack stilled. "Ethan? Do you know him?"

She nodded. "Actually, I met him in a geology class last year. I was surprised to see him in town."

"I didn't realize you two knew each other."

"Not well. We went out a few times. Nothing serious. I'm going diving with him tomorrow."

Jack put his fork down too loudly. The mystery of the handsome stranger was solved. "You're going to dive together? Is that a good idea?"

She frowned. "Why wouldn't it be?"

"He's a suspect in a murder investigation."

"A suspect? You don't really think he killed his camera guy."

"It's a possibility."

"I promise I'll always keep my guard up."

He didn't return her smile. "It's a bad idea, Bobby."

She folded her arms. "Let's put it on the table. This isn't about your investigation. This is because you don't like me hanging out with someone else, isn't it?"

He took a sip of water to stall for a moment. "I don't like you muddying the waters when I'm working on a case."

She snorted. "Muddying the waters? You make me sound like some sort of dog, playing around in your pond."

"That's not what I meant. I just think you should know who you're going to be gallivanting around with."

"Sometimes I'm not even sure I know you." Her eyes

blazed as she stood and pushed her chair in. "Don't worry. I'll be very careful not to contaminate any evidence when I'm out in the ocean with Ethan. Thanks for dinner."

She grabbed her jacket. He heard her kiss Paul and wish him good night. The front door slammed. After a moment he followed, jogging down the front drive. "Bobby, wait. I'm sorry."

She was too far away to hear, or maybe too angry to turn around.

His gut told him Bobby should stay away from Ethan Ping. A stab of conscience made him wonder if it really was his gut. Or his heart.

8

Ruth's camera was cold in her hands as she took pictures of the sunrise over the wild Pacific. She told herself the extra money from the sale of the postcard photos would help with the ever-growing list of baby essentials. She was rationalizing, of course.

"What kind of mother is afraid to be around her own son? Lord, what kind of a mother will I be to this new child?" She whispered her prayer to the wind. The baby kicked, a fluttery butterfly feeling.

The minutes of this pregnancy ticked away in a blur. Was she really almost forty-eight and pregnant? Would she love the baby as she loved Bryce? Would it turn out the way it had with him? Monk would be there, by her side, but she knew from painful experience that nothing in life is a given.

Bryce was finding that out the hard way after losing his baby, his wife, and his job in the space of a year. He wasn't used to losing. She'd tried so hard to prevent him from feeling that sting as a child, she wasn't sure he would be able to weather it now.

The wind whipped her hair around into a frizzy ball. Through her camera lens the steel gray ocean was choppy, restless. A figure came into view along the cliff line. She could just make out the angular face of Dr. Soloski. His head was bent, shoulders hunched. She considered calling out to him, but the man was absorbed in his own thoughts, as engrossing as her own. He looked tired, perhaps from running away from Ellen Foots.

Her stomach rumbled, and she was suddenly ravenous. It was a cruel trick, as she knew the hunger would be replaced by morning sickness in a few hours. Morning sickness. What a misnomer. If it was confined to the morning hours she'd count herself lucky. In the past few months she hadn't dared leave home without an airsick bag in each pocket.

For the moment, she turned her thoughts to food. Her mind traveled back to Indigo Orson's cramped handwritten scrawls, and she picked up the binder she'd brought along, to read the next passage.

> These men ate poorly, scavenging whatever they could and trying to turn it into something, anything edible, until God tossed me onto their shores. They told me of a cactus stew they had tried to make after a traveler traded them some for fresh water. Not a one of them gave a thought to removing the prickles before they boiled it. The traveler gave them dried tortoise, too. Most had never seen a tortoise, alive or dead, but that did not stop them from eating every speck of it.
>
> It reminded me of the strange animals Señor Orson told of when he returned from Australia before our disastrous voyage on the Triton. If there were kangaroos in California, they would be hopping for their lives to escape the stew pot.
>
> Mostly the men were used to beans and more beans, seasoned with only a bit of salt, so anything different was a joy to them. Once Old Severus

brought me six abalone he'd pried off the rocks with an iron bar. What a sweet delight they made, fried up with a pat of butter.

With my precious remaining treasure, I baked a dozen biscuits and sold them. I earned enough to buy more flour, some dried chilies, and salt pork and a set of tin plates. There was a quantity of wild onion and garlic growing near our camp to which the men paid no mind, but I gathered as if it was manna. I even found a small patch of wild oregano, and happy I was to pick some, too. It will be a wonderful treat for the men to have their food with a dab of seasoning, though they would happily eat it plain.

They now regard me as a priceless addition to their camp and afford me whatever small luxuries they can, such as a bucket for hauling water and a woolen blanket. Patchy even provided me with a crude butter churn, though where he got it I shiver to consider. When I can lay my hands on some milk, the men will have their butter.

Before I finished soaking the beans and chilies they circled like hungry dogs.

"What is it?" a fellow by the name of Slack asked me. "Never mind," he said. "Don't care what it is. When can I eat it?"

By the time they returned from their long day at the river, the chili was done. At the risk of disclosing my gender, I made them wash their filthy hands before I served them.

It is an oddly exhilarating place here, in this

wild land. The work is backbreaking, sure enough,
but it's my work, fashioned with my own hands,
planned in my own mind and brought about by
the sweat of my brow. For the first time in my life,
I am beholden to no one but myself and my God. I
work to survive, sure enough, but I feel as though the
compensation I receive goes beyond the coins I collect.

I know these are heathen men, rough and
hardened. Ah, but it does my heart good to see
them fill their stomachs. Perhaps if I can ease the
ferocious hunger which gnaws at their bellies, God
can fill their souls and take away the gold fever
that reduces them to animals.

As she closed the binder, Ruth was seized with an overwhelming desire to cook. The supremely elemental need to nourish another person filled her. If she couldn't talk to Bryce, at least she could feed him. She stretched the light sweater over her belly and headed to town enjoying the sights and smells of early summer.

She stopped at Puzan's Grocery and filled her basket with onion, chili, sausage, and a bunch of Royland Lemmon's gorgeous herbs. She held the fragrant bunch of thyme to her nose and breathed in the smell of greenery and, she imagined, sorrow.

Though she knew it wasn't her fault Royland's son was a murderer, she had definitely had a hand in solving the crime, and it pained her to see the look of defeat in Royland's face since his child went to prison. She insisted on delivering the farmer's worm order personally once a month, and staying awhile on his farm to chat. She knew she would never think of Royland without feeling that odd mixture of pity and guilt.

As she shifted the binder of Indigo's writings to pull the grocery money out of her pocket, a slip of paper floated to the floor. The small blue note was cryptic: *P.max. 468c/470c*. With a confused frown, she pocketed the paper and headed home.

Monk waited in the kitchen with a cup of tea already steeping. After kissing her on her lips and both cheeks, he put out a roast beef sandwich for himself and a grilled cheese for her.

"I thought you'd be busy at the shop."

"Bobby's handling things for a while." His forehead creased. "Is something going on with her? She seems awfully quiet. Said she's going diving with that Ethan fellow after lunch."

"Ethan? I didn't know she knew him. I wonder what Jack thinks about that."

He raised an eyebrow. "I can imagine what he thinks. Ethan better not break any laws while he's in town, or he'll be thrown in the slammer with a life sentence."

They laughed.

"I hope they work things out," Ruth said. "They are good for each other."

"Just like us." Monk toasted her with a root beer. "I've been so busy since I got back we haven't talked much. So how are you doing, honey? With the baby and. . .everything?"

She took a deep breath and, seeing the sympathetic look on his kind face, burst into a shower of tears. He came around in front of her and squeezed her gently.

"What is it, Ruthy? What's wrong?"

"Everything," she wailed. "I'm fat and sick, and I didn't do a good job mothering the first time and I'm way too old to learn how to parent now."

He patted her back, her tears soaking his shirt front. "You are a good mother and you'll be a good mother to Junior, too. You're just going through a patch of worry now. The hormones aren't helping, I'll bet."

"But, Monk," she said, pulling away. "Bryce didn't want to be around me, ever. He always wanted to do things himself, and if he couldn't do something he asked Philip for help. I think I tried to do too much for him." Her voice dropped to a whisper. "I smothered him, spoiled him, and he's paying the price for it now."

Monk tipped her face to his and patted her tears away with a napkin. "Ruthy, there's one very important thing you're forgetting."

"What?"

"Where did he go when his life fell apart?"

She blinked. "He, he came—"

"Home to you," he finished.

She fed the worms their vegetable peelings and sprinkled the beds with a layer of hay. As usual, the gulls jostled around, their beaks poking into the dark soil, the fanning of their wings creating a breeze on her legs.

"No, you don't, Rutherford." She pushed him away, then sidestepped the eager Grover. "Here's your lunch." She tossed cubes of stale bread and bits of apples to the feathery swarm. Their loud squawks filled the cool afternoon air with discordant music. She couldn't help but smile at the greedy horde. The sight always brought back a fond memory of Phillip. For a long time, she'd pushed the memories away, but now she savored them, like looking at old photos in a scrapbook.

A laugh made her turn.

"Those are the strangest pets," Bryce said, arms folded across his chest. "Most people would choose a dog or cat."

"They are strange companions. They don't heel, they can't fetch, and only Martha comes when called. Weird is an understatement, but your father chose them for us, so that's that."

He nodded. "I was on my way to the beach and I ran into that blond lady, the filmmaker. What's her name?"

"Sandra Marconi."

"That's the one. She said she needs to talk to you. She'll come by later."

"I wonder what that's all about." Absently she fingered the paper in her pocket and pulled it out. "Bryce, does this note mean anything to you?"

He frowned at the scrap. "No. Not really. Looks like some kind of foreign language. Where did you get it?"

"I found it in the notebook Sandra gave me."

"Oh. Maybe she can tell you then." They lapsed into silence. Bryce shifted from one foot to the other, dark eyes fixed on the swarming birds as they finished up their meal.

"Who was that other lady? The one with the cap that came for worms last night?"

"Her name is Roxie Trotter. Why?"

"No particular reason. She looks familiar to me, but I don't know where from." He watched the birds bob and weave across the yard.

Ruth wondered as she looked at Bryce's thin face. Who was this grown man? What were his passions and dreams? He might be a total stranger who wandered in off the street, for all she knew about him. She wanted to talk, to free them from the distance that yawned between them, but she couldn't think of a way to do it.

Ruth brushed off her hands. She spoke before she had a chance to think about the logic of her plan. "I'm going to make chili."

Bryce raised an eyebrow. "Really? I figured spicy food would make you sick. Roslyn always had heartburn. I used to keep a roll of antacids in every jacket I owned so she'd have some when she needed them."

Her heart ached to see the flitter of pain on his face. "It does and it will, but for now, I'm making chili."

"Okay." He trailed behind her into the kitchen. "Maybe I could give you a hand."

Her heart skipped a beat, and she fought to keep her voice level as they entered the kitchen. "That would be great. Can you get out my chili pot from down there? Bending over makes my head spin like a top." Without a word he pulled the pot from the low cupboard. She handed him the dry beans. He sat at the table, his head bent, sorting them into precise piles and removing the occasional stone, like a miser poring over gold pieces.

She chopped an onion and peeled the garlic.

Bryce poured his sorted beans back into the pot and added water. It was quiet for a while except for the sound of her knife on the cutting board. Bryce retrieved the herbs from the fridge.

"Remember earthquake cake?"

She started, her mouth open in a momentary *O* of surprise. "Earthquake cake? That awful chocolate thing we spackled together with frosting for Dad's birthday?"

"Yeah. Dad said it was the best cake he ever had."

Against all reason, her eyes filled. Bryce remembered earthquake cake. "He would say that about every cake we ever made."

"Yeah. He was a natural-born optimist." Bryce fingered the leathery skin of the chilies. "I miss him."

"I miss him, too."

"Do you. . .ever visit his grave?"

"Of course, honey, often. Monk and I go together every now and then. We pray and leave flowers. Sometimes I take the birds. I think your father would have liked that."

"I think you're right."

Bryce's cell phone rang, and he went in the other room to answer it.

Ruth tried not to listen. His comments were short. The sound of the bubbling pot did not quite drown out the angry cadence of his words.

When he returned, his brow was furrowed, and he looked much older than he had a moment before. "Roslyn needs me to sign some papers so we can put the house on the market."

"Oh, I see. That's. . .sad. Isn't it?"

He shrugged. "Might as well sell it. It's not my home anymore. I need some air. I'm going for a walk."

Ruth watched him through the kitchen window as he left the house, studying the flagstone path beneath his feet as he headed to the street.

She looked around at her own small house, the scratched tile counter, the smooth wooden floor, drapes that fluttered in the breeze from the open window. Those walls had been home to two husbands and a little boy at one point. Sweet little Cootchie had listened to her read many a story here. Soon it would be home to another child. Through all the heartbreak of losing Phillip, and the struggle with Bryce, it had never stopped being home to her.

"How very blessed I am, Lord. Thank You for reminding me."

She made sure the beans were simmering, starting the process to fill their bellies, praying that God would fill Bryce's soul. As she hummed a tune, marveling that the scent of onions and garlic hadn't sent her stomach on a roller-coaster ride, Ruth didn't notice the small clink as her wedding ring slipped off the counter and into the sink. She started the disposal, and the horrible clanking noise made her slam off the switch.

She fished around in the drain and came up with the object.

The plain gold band was twisted and scarred.

With trembling fingers she held the band to her chest and cried.

An hour later Ruth ushered Sandra into the kitchen in the late afternoon. The fragrance of cooking chili filled every nook and cranny of the house.

"That smells wonderful," Sandra said.

"Thank you. I was inspired by Indigo Orson, only she made hers without the benefit of a sink or cutting boards. The miners didn't seem to mind."

Sandra laughed, making her eyes sparkle. "She was an amazing woman."

Ruth gestured for Sandra to sit. "How did you learn of her?"

"I was doing some research on steamships, and I came across her name on a passenger list. I was lucky enough to find her journal buried in the archives. It was a miracle really. The papers were mixed in with a pile of receipts and such, ready to be disposed of."

"Are you a history major then?"

Her face broke into a wide smile. "Not anymore, but I sure miss it. I love everything about it, the thrill of finding a new connection between the past and the present, poring over old maps. I even love the musty smell of old books. I'm a history geek for sure."

Ruth laughed. "You'll have to go visit Ellen Foots, our librarian. She's ferocious about her passion for research materials. I think she was a history major, too."

"Actually, when the project is done, I'm going to switch gears and work on a master's in business."

"Really? Why?"

Sandra tugged on a strand of her white blond hair. "Sadly, I learned that you really can't pay the bills too effectively with a history degree. I've had to look for other means. I've done everything from flipping burgers to stocking shelves." She flexed her knee. "I tore my ACL last year, and the surgery for that cost me a bundle, let me tell you. My surgeon sends me little pink notes every month reminding me I'm not finished paying for my bionic knee. They're not valentines, I can tell you."

"Was the surgery a success?"

She sighed, rubbing her knee thoughtfully. "I guess, but the body never really does recover from some things."

Ruth remembered the stretch marks that snaked like snail trails over her protruding belly after Bryce was born. What permanent marks would this later-in-life baby leave on her body? "I'm afraid you're right about that."

"Are you feeling okay? Is the pregnancy going okay and everything?" Sandra looked uneasy. "Oh, maybe that's too personal to ask. I'm sorry if I was rude."

"Not at all. I'm the topic of conversation at dinner tables all over Finny. As far as I can tell, everything is right on track," Ruth said. "I've got one of those big appointments coming up, the pregnancy milestones that make you stay up at night and worry."

Her smile was sympathetic. "I've never been pregnant, but I've had plenty of those nights, especially lately." Sandra glanced at her watch. "The reason I stopped by is I need the binder, with Indigo's notes."

"Oh, really? Are we going to quit filming?"

"No, no. In fact, we need to speed things up. The long-range weather gurus are forecasting a storm by week's end. I need to, um, make some notes. I'll give it back tomorrow. I promise." She held up three fingers in a Girl Scout salute.

"Sure. I'll go get it." Ruth passed the nursery on her way down the hall, wondering for the umpteenth time if it should be blue or pink. The day before, she'd decided on the palest of yellows, but that was yesterday. Maybe she should just ask the doctor and get it over with. Maybe it would help to make it all more real, somehow.

She retrieved the binder and remembered the cryptic piece of paper. On impulse, she jotted down the numbers on a pad before she replaced the note among other pages and returned to the kitchen.

Sandra looked up from the chili pot. She blushed and replaced the lid. "Oh, sorry. I hope you don't mind. It's been awhile since I smelled a good home-cooked chili. My dad makes a mean pot, but I haven't been home in a few years."

"Where is home?"

"Montana. He moved us up there after my mom took off."

"Oh. That's too bad. About your mother, I mean."

She shrugged and took the binder from Ruth. "It happens. I was only three so I don't remember her much. My brother was ten so it really threw him for a loop. He's dead now. Car wreck."

Ruth saw grief in the woman's face. "I'm so sorry."

"Me, too. He was a great big brother." Sandra turned to go. "I'd better go. Nice talking to you, Mrs. Budge."

"Call me Ruth. I'll save you some chili when it's done."

"That would be super." Sandra gazed into her face for a long moment. "You're going to be a good mother, I'll bet."

Ruth felt a warmth in her cheeks. "It's what I'm praying for."

<hr />

Just before midnight Ruth wandered into the kitchen, which still smelled of chili in spite of leaving the windows open for several hours. Though she had eaten two bowls earlier, the smell now made her stomach quiver. She held her breath and poured a glass of milk. It surprised her to find Indigo Orson's journal on the sideboard with a note.

> *Mom, Sandra saw me in town and asked me to return this to you. You were asleep when I got home, so I put it here. I ate more of the chili for a snack. It is good stuff. Bryce.*

Smiling, she sat on the sofa to sip her milk and thumb through the photocopied journal pages. There were no changes that she could detect. Then she checked the front inside flap.

"I take that back. There is one change," she muttered to herself.

The cryptic numbered note was gone.

9

Jack waited until ten thirty in the morning to go to the library. He knew Ellen Foots attended a Thursday People and Paws meeting at the high school gym on Fridays at that time so he figured he was safe from the prying giantess.

He made his way to the nonfiction section and hunted until he found it. *Beginning Scuba*. Perfect. Three hundred fifty pages of details that would open up a whole new undersea world or condemn him to a watery grave. As he went to the front desk, he wondered why anyone would choose to strap on a bottle of air and sink themselves on purpose. It was just an unnatural thing to do. Plenty of people did it, however, he thought with a grimace, including Ethan Ping, who he'd heard was escorting Bobby on another dive that very afternoon. He slapped his library card down on the front desk more forcefully than he intended.

Ellen emerged from the back, her hair poking out from a headband that struggled to hold it all in.

His heart sank a notch. "Ellen. I thought you were at your People and Paws meeting."

"Had to cancel. Maude had a dental emergency." Her heavy brows furrowed. "At least, that's what she says. I think she's just trying to get her claws into Dr. Soloski. She's on him like pudding skin."

The guy must feel like the last hunk of meat at a tiger convention. "That's too bad."

Ellen scanned the bar code. "You're going to learn how to scuba dive?"

"Uh, no. Just a little background for the investigation."

Her face grew thoughtful for a moment and then resolved into a scowl. "You know, I'm going over there right now to check on Maude. If she's got a cracked crown, I'm Nefertiti."

He hid a smile as he took the book.

———

An hour later the book remained on the front seat of his car and Maude was in his office. She still wore the paper bib from the dentist visit.

"It's stalking, I'm telling you. Or invasion of privacy. Imagine, bursting in on a patient's dental exam. Why, poor Dr. Soloski could have slipped and put his hook through my lip or something."

We couldn't be that lucky. "But it all ended well, didn't it? Dr. Soloski was able to fix your crown after all, wasn't he?"

"Crown? Oh, it wasn't cracked after all. Silly of me."

Jack looked at Maude's tight bun and her squared shoulders. The woman didn't have a silly molecule in her spindly body. He reined in an exasperated sigh. "I'm not going to arrest Ellen, Maude, so is there anything else I can do for you?"

Maude's cheeks colored. "Stalkers. Bodies washing up on beaches. People slinking around at night, and what does the Finny police department do about it? Nothing. Not a pinky lifted to help out the citizens of this town. Shocking. I tell you it's shocking."

Jack sifted through the rambling. "Who's slinking around at night?"

"Not that you'd be interested at all, but there's been a boat out the last two nights. Late. Around two o'clock in the morning. My insomnia has been troubling me so I happen to notice them. No one has legitimate business out on the water at that hour, now do they?"

"Who was it?"

"I don't know. My binoculars weren't strong enough, but the boat looked like Roxie's. Whoever it was had to be up to no good." Maude's black eyes widened under her pencil-drawn brows. "I know. I bet it was Ellen. She was probably dumping a body over the side."

Jack looked at her. "Whose body would she be dumping exactly?"

"Oh, I don't know. You're the police. Aren't you supposed to figure things like that out? You did go to investigator school, didn't you? I know she's got a motive somewhere in her shady past."

Nate poked his head in. "Hey, Maude. There's a group of women roaming the town looking for you. They say they're ready for their visit to the movie site."

Maude shot out of the chair so fast she knocked it over. "Oh my. Is it that time already? Business is hopping. I've got another tour group to lead. Excuse me, gentlemen."

Nate nodded. "You might want to take off the bib first."

She sniffed and swept out of the room, her cast thumping against the floor in a rapid staccato.

Jack slumped in relief. "Thanks for the rescue. I'm promoting you to the upstairs office."

Nate uprighted the chair and settled in. "Great. If

we should ever build an upstairs, I'll remind you of that. Louella called."

His heart skipped a bit as it always did when Paul's babysitter called. "Is everything okay?"

"You bet. She said to remind you the butterfly tea party is this afternoon at the preschool and the pleasure of your attendance is required."

He felt a twinge of guilt because he had not remembered what the twelve thirty entry in his PDA was for. "Right. Butterfly tea. I'm on it."

"Do you have to bring your own butterflies?"

"Funny. You shouldn't be handing out grief here. I remember you making an Easter bonnet when Janet couldn't make it to the triplet's Sunday school party."

"It was a fine looking bonnet."

"Can't argue with that. I particularly liked the way you drew handcuffs on the side. What do you hear about Reggie?"

"He's still dead."

"Uh-huh. And?"

Nate pulled his mustache. "And he participated in some questionable treasure hunting."

"What kind?"

"The kind when you salvage artifacts off a historical wreck and sell them for profit."

Jack sat up straighter. "A historical wreck?"

"Mmhmm. Worked for a man last name of Skylar. Ring any bells?"

"My bells are ringing. Did he have an arrest record for this hunting?"

"Nope. Turns out maritime law is a bit foggy. According

to the Abandoned Ship Act, the government owns all shipwrecks in state waters out to three miles on the Atlantic and Pacific coasts. The particular wreck in question was slightly over that distance so Skylar hired a crew to pick it clean. There wasn't much there worth salvaging, but they got themselves on the Coast Guard watch list."

"Strange coincidence that a man of the same name is funding this little voyage through history, right off our humble coast."

"Isn't it, though? Think the *Triton* was carrying any good cargo? Maybe there was something buried under all that coal."

"Might be interesting to find out."

Nate checked his watch. "Eleven thirty, boss. When do you have to report for butterfly duty?"

"Soon, but I've got something to do first."

Jack walked partway up the steep trail, stopping behind the gnarled cypress. Down below he could see them making their slow exit from the water. Bobby's figure was slight and smaller than Ethan's, the only way he could tell the two wet-suited people apart. On the beach they began to strip off their gear. He couldn't make out their words, but Bobby's peal of laughter came through loud and clear.

His stomach muscles clenched when Ethan held Bobby's arm while she removed her flippers. There had to be some reason this guy should be in jail. He'd make sure to find out what it was.

Ethan shouldered his gear and, with a wave, headed

away toward town. Bobby pulled off her wet suit. She sat on the sand in her one-piece bathing suit, gazing out at the ocean. Jack watched her black hair dance in the breeze, and he unconsciously took a step forward, wishing he could join her on the warm beach. He thought better of it and leaned back. The rocky ground under his feet gave way, and he tumbled down the slope.

⁓

The sun was warm on his face. Fingers stroked his cheek, coaxing his eyes into opening. He blinked.

Bobby's eyes were wide, anxious. "Are you all right?"

He blinked again. "You smell nice."

She raised an eyebrow. "No, I don't. I smell like seaweed."

He was relieved to find no trace of anger on her face from their last meeting. "No, you smell like a great cup of coffee."

She laughed. "Okay. I know your nose is working. Did you hurt anything else?"

He shifted his limbs. Aside from dozens of pain pricks, all the parts seemed functional. He sat up and waited for the sparks to stop dancing in his head.

Bobby looked into his eyes. "Pupils look normal, but I'd better call an ambulance anyway."

He grabbed her wrist as she started to go. "No. I'm okay. Just, just stay here for a minute."

She settled back next to him. "Do you want to tell me why you were spying on me?"

"Spying? I wasn't spying. I was out for a walk, and I

saw you down there with College Boy."

"His name is Ethan, and I don't buy that for a minute."

Jack bit back a sarcastic remark. He didn't want to make an idiot of himself again.

She gently brushed the gravel bits out of his hair and ran soft fingers along his head. The feel of her wrapped his insides in a flood of warmth.

He cleared his throat. "Did you enjoy your dive?"

"Sure." She continued to watch his face. "I love diving. Beautiful kelp beds out there."

"Yeah. I've been considering trying it out."

"Trying what out?"

"Diving."

"You?" She laughed. "That's a good one."

He sat up straighter. "What's so funny about that?"

"Nothing. Diving is great. You'll love it, but don't go alone."

"Does Ethan dive alone?"

"I don't think so. Why? Oh, I know. You think he's up to no good, right?"

"You said it, I didn't."

She stood, brushing sand from her legs. "Let's not have another argument here, shall we? You're not going to use me to dig up dirt on Ethan. He's a nice guy, Jack."

"Then why is he in partnership with a modern-day pirate?"

"What?"

"The guy funding his quote unquote research is a man who steals treasure from shipwrecks that belong to the state."

"Hard way to make a living." Her eyes narrowed. "Besides,

there's one problem with your pat theory."

"What's that?"

"The *Triton* carried a giant boatload of coal. Not coins, jewelry, or even silver. It was a cargo ship with very few civilian passengers. So there isn't anything on that boat except maybe a few trinkets of interest to historians."

He looked out at the waves. "Maybe, maybe not."

"Let's get real here. Your case is weak and you know it. Ethan has nothing to gain from that wreck except historical information, which is exactly what he said he was after in the first place."

Jack sniffed and looked away. "My gut tells me he's not just here for the history."

"Sometimes people really are what they seem to be." She picked up her air tanks and wet suit. "I'm gonna go now. Are you sure you're all right?"

"Absolutely."

He heaved himself from the ground and stood upright before a wave of dizziness made him stagger. Bobby dropped her gear and grabbed him. "Absolutely, huh?" She tucked a shoulder under his arm and helped him walk.

Jack leaned on her. "Why are you helping? I thought you were mad at me."

"I am mad at you. And you know why I'm helping."

"I do?"

She stopped and sighed deeply. Her fingers wound around his neck, and she kissed him full on the mouth. "Because I love you, you idiot."

The kiss ended too soon. He was momentarily over-whelmed with joy, dizzy and not from the fall. She loved him. He should open his mouth and tell her how he felt. He should. He should.

She waited a fraction of a second longer and then dropped her gaze to the sand. "That's what I thought. Come on. Let's get you back to your car."

They reached the parking lot, and he brushed off his clothes, feeling her disappointment, heavy as his own. "Bobby—"

She shook her head. "Don't say a word. You'd better go home and take a shower."

"I wish I could, but I'm late for a party."

"What kind of party?"

"A butterfly tea party. We're making tissue flowers."

Though her face still wore the signs of sadness, Bobby tilted her face to the sun and laughed.

Paul wrinkled his nose in concentration as he folded the tissue into pleats. He poofed the delicate yellow paper and a smile lit his face as he held it up for his father. "See? It's a flower."

"Nice, buddy. Great job." Jack felt the curious glances from the room full of moms. He was scratched and bruised from his fall. The muscles in his back ached. The classroom was filled with mothers and children, expertly making tissue flower bouquets and pasting minute plastic butterflies on them.

"Now you." Paul slid the pipe cleaners and a handful of tissue at his father.

"Oh, Dad's not so good at this kind of thing. Why

don't you make some more? Yours are super."

His face fell. "You're supposed to do it."

Jack couldn't stand that look for another second. "Well, I'll give it a try. Let's see, how did you fold it?" As he fiddled with the wads of tissue, Jack thought about Lacey. She would have made perfect flowers. *But she's not here*, he thought angrily, *she's dead, so I'm stuck making tissue flowers that look like someone chewed them and spit them out.*

The paper would not cooperate under his clumsy fingers. He produced a sad, crumpled mass, like a blossom trodden under the weight of many feet.

Paul looked at it. "That doesn't look good, Daddy."

I'm not good, Paul. I'm an idiot and a coward to boot. Why hadn't he told Bobby he loved her? He could feel love in every pore of his body, but he hadn't said the words to anyone besides Paul since Lacey died. He loved Lacey. And he loved Bobby, but he continued to let her down. No wonder she was scuba diving with other guys. "Sorry, son. I'll try again."

Someone took the pipe cleaner and tissue from his hands and slid into the chair next to him. Bobby folded the paper into the perfect tissue bloom. She smiled. "There you go, Paul. Isn't that the best flower you ever saw?"

"Oh yeah," the boy yelled. "That's great, Bobby."

She nodded. "Yes, it is. Get me a butterfly and more tissue, and we'll finish this bouquet." She lowered her voice to a whisper. "Ours will be the best one at this party."

With a giggle, Paul leaped out of the chair to fetch more supplies.

Jack looked at her. "I thought you were mad at me."

"I am mad at you. You're a jealous cretin who has no

business telling me who I can and cannot see. And you are also a dismal failure at arts and crafts." She flipped her bobbed hair out of her face. "I, on the other hand, made six thousand tissue flowers for a Cinco de Mayo float so I'm a professional. I figured Paul could use a hand."

Jack looked into her black eyes and saw love shining there, love that he didn't deserve. "He sure could." *And so could I.*

10

*G*od has sent me a soul even more wretched than I was the day I washed up on this shore. He's a Chinese boy, name of Hui, which means splendor, I have since discovered. I found him one day, hidden under a broken wagon. I wouldn't have noticed him at all if he hadn't sneezed.

His mother died of fever when he was born, and his father came to California to work the gold fields. Of course, being Chinese, they were forced to work the claims that had already been stripped clean. Hui was one of a group of fifty Chinese men and boys that came to Gold Country only to find themselves banned from the most current diggings. Gradually they dispersed, looking for meager leftovers from already bare land. The fortunate ones with some money to front were able to open laundries and restaurants and the occasional store in town.

Hui and his father were not so lucky. They camped in a cave halfway up the side of the mountain until some white men caught Hui's father panning in a forbidden place. They beat him to death. Hui buried him as best he could and survived by snitching food from the campsites at night. They caught him once, and he has a bruised face and a broken finger to show for his narrow escape. I am reminded that these men remain more animal than human sometimes.

I found him, one midnight, hiding under that wagon with scraps he'd taken from the rubbish heap, bone thin, black eyes huge with terror. I don't speak Chinese, but Hui speaks a good bit of English that he learned from listening on the ship voyage from China. He didn't need to say a word, though, for me to see the desperation on his young face. I don't suppose he's much older than ten years, though he isn't exactly certain of his birth date because the Chinese calendar is much different than ours. Somehow I persuaded him to come to my tent and eat some dried meat and berries. The food was meager, but he devoured it in a thrice before he ate the three biscuits I'd been saving for breakfast.

We made him sort of a bed out of a blanket and some burlap bags. Though the night was hot, he trembled in a miserable state until he finally fell into an exhausted slumber. That was three nights ago, and he still shivers when darkness comes, rolled into a ball on the floor of my tent.

He lives in terror of being killed, and goodness knows he has reason for his fear. Like the Mexicans, the Chinese are despised in the mining camps, lower than dogs. The first morning Hui peeked out of my tent, Slack saw him and came running with a shovel. I stood between them and raised my ladle like a sword.

"This boy is mine, Señor. Any one of you who lays a hand to him will never eat from my pot again. I'll see you starve first."

That made them temper their anger. Losing

their chance at real food proved stronger than the need for foolish violence. They look at him with cruel eyes, but no one has dared to touch the boy. Nonetheless he stays at my side every minute and helps me with the cooking and cleaning up. He is very good at tending the fire, making sure it never goes out or burns too hot to scorch the soup. He gathered leaves from somewhere and brewed them into a sort of tea which we have both found to be of comfort on these cold mornings.

I believe Hui knows that I am a woman, but he will keep my secret, I am sure of it. We are both strangers here, and God has put us together for His good purpose. I hold His promise next to my heart for both our sakes: " 'For I know the thoughts I think toward you,' saith the LORD, 'thoughts of peace, and not of evil, to give you an expected end.' "

Ruth eased down onto the sofa, trying to keep down the glass of water she'd drunk. *The plans I have for you.* She groaned, clasping a hand to her aching back. A later-than-midlife pregnancy and a son whose world was crumbling sure seemed like the definition of calamity. What was the future going to look like? A decade ago she thought it was a life with Phillip, the man she adored, but that was not to be. And what should she hope for? For a long life with her husband and a new baby? She had already cherished that hope a lifetime ago. God's plan seemed as foggy to her as the Finny coastline in the spring. The terror of it all swept over her again.

Alva knocked, and she clambered to her feet to let hi

in. He fished the abalone shell from his cavernous pocket. "I need yer help, sweet cheeks. Can you keep it safe fer me? That thievin' dentist may aim to swipe it back."

Ruth squelched a smile. "I'm sure he's over the loss of his business card holder by now."

"Maybe, maybe not." Alva put the shell on the kitchen counter and filled it with apples from the fruit bowl. "There. Hidden in plain sight and all. I stowed my other treasures in separate locations so as to foil any criminal masterminds. Are you ready to go to town?"

"Yes, Alva. I've gone to the bathroom three times and managed to swallow those horrible prenatal pills. I'm ready to face the afternoon."

"Okey doke. It's free sample day at the Buns Up Bakery. You and me can swipe a bunch of them sugar cookies. You got big pockets?"

The thought of food made her stomach heave. "I'll head to the jewelers. You can stop at Buns Up if you want to." Ruth took her mangled ring from the counter.

"Well, whaddja do to it anyway?" Alva squinted a rheumy eye at the squished band of gold. "It looks like ya done run it over or something."

Ruth pocketed the metal, feeling the tears threaten again. "I dropped it down the sink when the disposal was running. What a klutz."

Alva patted her hand. "Oh now, don't you pay it no never mind. One time I dropped Daddy's teeth in the dog food. Fluffers ate it up afore I could fish it out. We had to wait two days until it made an appearance again. Daddy twerent happy about it at all."

She pulled a sweater over her protruding stomach and

gave up trying to button it. "I don't feel so bad about the ring then."

Ruth and Alva linked arms as they headed toward Main Street. The air was warm, full of the promise of a hot summer ahead. The potted hydrangeas that lined the sidewalks were dotted with blooms, and the bougainvillea climbing the cracked stucco walls of the hotel seemed to vibrate with a wave of color.

Alva handed her a bag of candy corn. "Vegetables, so the baby don't come out with two heads or anything."

She sucked on a sweet triangle.

"I've been reading this book that Petey Fisk loaned me about babies. What's this about them havin' a soft spot on their heads?"

"It's only for a while, until their skulls fuse together."

He looked alarmed. "Sakes. You think we ought to get the little dickens a helmet until the fusion thing is done?"

It felt so good to laugh. "Let's see how it goes, okay?"

Alva nodded. "Whatever you say, sweet cheeks." He stopped long enough at the bakery to load his pockets with cookie samples. Ruth stayed outside. They continued their stroll until they came to the shop. With a gallant flourish he opened the door of Finny Jewelers, and she headed inside.

Roxie stood at the glass counter with Stew Barnes, Finny's only jeweler. Stew looked up. "Hello, Ruth. Good to see you. Come on in, and I'll be with you in a minute."

Ruth nodded. She wandered around the cases and listened in with only a sliver of guilt.

"Last time you gave me ten per shell," Roxie said.

"Last time I needed them for a display. This time I'm

just being nice." He piled the stack of three abalone shells on the counter and measured them with a ruler.

"They're legal," she snapped. "I know the rules. They're all bigger than seven inches."

Stew raised an eyebrow. "And you didn't harvest them using scuba gear?"

Roxie's cheeks reddened. "Of course I didn't. Now, are you going to pay me or not?"

Alva's eyebrows zinged up. "Pay her? You gonna pay her for the shells? Without the pearls in 'em?"

The jeweler put down his ruler. "Pearls don't come from abalone, Alva. They come from oysters. I use the shells for display because they're pretty and you can fit a whole necklace inside."

The old man's eyes darted around in thought. "I got me a sweet shell from the dentist. How much you give me fer it?"

Stew's eyebrow arched. "You got a shell from the dentist? What happened to lollipops?"

"He ain't that sort of a dentist. He said lollipops would give me the decay, so I picked the shell instead. What'll you give me?"

Stew scratched the bald patch on the top of his head. "As I was just saying, I have enough shells. I'm using them for a new pearl display, and I've got plenty. I'm not going to buy any more from Roxie, either."

Alva chuckled. "Oh, that's what you say now, but you wait till you see the beauty I've got. That shell is tops."

Roxie grabbed a black bag from the counter. "I guess we're finished here."

Alva tugged on her shirt. "Where'd you find them

shells? I'd like to get me some sweet abalones for sure. A wad of butter and a smack of garlic." He licked his lips.

"Go find them yourself," she snarled, walking to the corner to repack her shells.

Alva didn't miss a beat. "Right then. Say, Mr. Barnes. You got any cardboard boxes out back? Bobby said she'd show me and Paul how to make a rocket."

"Sure thing. Help yourself to whatever is out there."

"Be back in a jiff. I need an extra strong one for the life support systems." The old man hobbled out the back door.

Stew opened his mouth to answer, but Alva was gone. "His elevator doesn't quite reach the penthouse, does it?"

Ruth laughed. "Probably not, but I'm not convinced mine does, either. Maybe sanity is overrated."

He shrugged. "What can I do for you, Ruth?"

She held out the mashed gold band. "Can it be saved? Tell me it can, Stew. Please. "

He turned the ring around, squinting at it from all angles. "Might be easier just to get a new one."

"I can't. It's my wedding band." She swallowed hard.

"Well, let me take it in the back and have a closer look. Be back in a minute."

Ruth wandered over to the glass counters. The pearl display was lovely. Pastel colored orbs nestled on satin set against iridescent abalone shells. The colors winked and shimmered in the sunlight that streamed through the window. She looked at the placard standing on an easel in the case. There was a picture of an enormous, misshapen white blob. The tiny writing underneath read *Pinctada maxima*, 14 lbs. The thing was the size of a small dog she used to own.

A voice startled her. "Now that's a big pearl," Dr. Soloski said.

He wore yet another jogging suit.

She nodded, peering again at the picture of the massive pearl. "Wouldn't work too well in a ring."

They stared at the luminous spread. "I've always kind of admired oysters, though." Dr. Soloski peered through his wire-rimmed glasses. "They take something bad, an irritation really, and make it into something wonderful. That's what a pearl is, a protective coating around an annoying bit of sand or grit."

Ruth looked at a teardrop-shaped pink pearl. "I never thought of it that way. It's amazing that someone would dive down and get these things from the bottom of the ocean. I sure wouldn't go to such trouble, even for a fourteen-pound pearl."

"Me neither. Diving is not for me."

Ruth looked up to see Roxie peering closely at the dentist. "They didn't have to dive far for those. Most of them are cultured pearls, a thin layer of nacre around a manmade center."

Stew emerged from the back in time to hear Roxie's comment. "There's nothing wrong with cultured pearls. Hello, Dr. Soloski. I've got your order ready. Would you like that gift wrapped?"

"That would be nice." Dr. Soloski followed Stew back to the counter. Ruth casually eased closer to watch Stew package a gold heart locket in a small box.

Dr. Soloski was buying someone a nice gift. Was it a love token? Had he finally succumbed to the not-so-subtle charms of Ellen? Or Maude? Her thoughts were interrupted when Alva barreled back into the store, hauling two enormous cardboard boxes.

"These are going to make a fine rocket. Hey. Who's the locket for? My auntie Mim had a necklace like that. Carried a picture of her wart in it. Looked just like Gerald Ford. The wart, not Auntie Mim."

Alva caught sight of Dr. Soloski and shrank back behind his cargo.

"Hello, Alva. Are you going to come and see me again soon? We've still got that cracked filling to take care of."

"I hear the phone ringing. Gotta go." Alva pushed out the door, knocking Roxie's bag out of her hands in the process.

Ruth halted a rolling abalone shell with her foot. She helped Roxie pick up the half dozen bumpy runaways. They felt oddly light in her hands, the outsides rough and ugly, the insides an iridescent rainbow of colors. She marveled that God could create such a perfect beauty and hide it in the roughest of exteriors.

"These are so interesting, Roxie. Too bad Stew can't use them all. Did you get them from around here?"

"Yeah. I'm done, though. I've met my limit for the year."

"Really?"

"It's three per day maximum, twenty-four per year."

"That's pretty strict."

"Abalone grows slowly, and it's been exploited for commercial harvest. In the past people basically decimated the population and didn't leave enough stock to regenerate. Some species are practically extinct now."

Ruth watched Roxie close the bag. A suspicion

crowded into her mind. "I guess some restaurants would pay top dollar for good abalone. That might encourage people to bend the rules a bit."

Roxie straightened, eyes narrowed. "I guess it might. But some of us have principles, no matter how broke we are. There are things in this world more precious than money." She shoved the door open and left.

Dr. Soloski finished his purchase and said good-bye.

Stew wrote up an order slip. "The good news is I can fix it. The bad news is it's gonna cost you fifty dollars and it will take a few days."

Relief swept through her like an ocean current. "Oh, thank you so much. I'm not in a hurry. Call me when you're ready for me to pick it up."

Outside the shop, Ruth felt suddenly exhausted and sank down on a bench on the sidewalk. The first hurdle of the day was behind her. She checked her watch. In half an hour came another hurdle that took the very breath out of her. It was all she could do to heave herself to her feet when Monk showed up. He kissed her twice, leaving her breathless.

"Ready, Ruthy?"

Her insides went cold. "No. No, I'm not ready. I can't do it. What if—?" She could not give voice to the fear.

He squeezed her hand. "No, what ifs. We will eat anything dished out to us."

She managed a faint laugh. "Is that a bit of catering wisdom?"

His wide face split into a grin. "Nah. That's navy."

"Really, though. I mean, it wouldn't be totally unexpected if, you know, there was something, not right. At my age and all." She looked at the scuffed toes of her walking shoes.

Monk stopped and turned to face her. "Now you listen to me. I don't want to hear any more of this 'at your age' talk. There's a reason that God blessed us with this at this time in our lives. He knows what He's doing. We are going to operate on the notion that this baby is in tiptop condition until we are told otherwise. If there is anything unusual to face, we will do it with His help." He resumed their march to the clinic, tucking her arm in his.

On the way she studied the set to his chin, marveling at how very blessed she was to have such a truly good man to love. He didn't fool her, though. The worry line between his brows spoke volumes. He'd been on edge about this doctor's appointment, too. It hadn't occurred to her to wonder about his fears and misgivings in the face of her own constant emotional ebb and flow. She squeezed his hand as they entered.

They waited an interminable amount of time, it seemed to Ruth, sandwiched in the holding area between Monk on one side and a young expectant mother on the other. Though she tried not to stare, she couldn't help but notice the woman's smooth face and her hand that lay across her belly. It was soft, unspotted, nicely manicured, and decorated with two rings. She read a magazine called *Yoga and You*.

Ruth tucked her own hands under her thighs. She would not dream of encasing her body in spandex and setting foot in an exercise class. Her bladder felt like a tightly stretched balloon. She whispered to her husband, "I drank all the water I was supposed to, but I've just got to go to the bathroom or I'm going to explode right here in this waiting room."

"Go ahead. I'll cover for you," Monk whispered back. "If anybody asks, I'll say you stepped out for a breath of fresh air."

When she got back, a smock-covered lady named Mai ushered them into a waiting room and helped Ruth don her putty gray hospital gown. Ruth lay on her back while the woman applied warm goo to her stomach and pressed a wand gently against her abdomen.

"Don't press too hard," Ruth advised. "Even though I snuck in a trip to the bathroom, I'm so full of water we might have a breach in the dam."

Mai smiled. "Don't worry, Ruth. I've seen plenty in this exam room. Just try to relax. This won't take long." She swiveled the wand around the vicinity of Ruth's belly button. Her brows drew together in concentration.

A full minute passed.

She lifted the instrument away and then pressed it again to Ruth's skin.

The frown increased and another minute crept by.

"What—what is it?" Ruth felt a cold fear clamp down on her heart. "Is there something wrong?"

Monk rose from his seat by the video screen. He gripped Ruth's hand so hard, he squashed her fingers together. "Tell us."

Mai put the wand on a paper and held up a finger, a bright smile on her face. "I need to get the doctor for a quick consult. Don't worry. Be right back." Mai scurried out the door.

The silence closed around them in a smothering blanket of fear. "Oh, Monk. There's something wrong."

Her hands went icy cold.

He brushed the hair out of her face. "We don't know that. She's a technician but she's not allowed to comment on the ultrasound results. Didn't you tell me that? Even if, well, in no circumstance is she supposed to give her two cents."

Her head was too muddled to speak. She thought inexplicably of Cootchie, her pseudo granddaughter, and the moment, the one horrific moment, when she looked around and Cootchie was gone, snatched right from under her nose. Tears crowded the corner of her eyes. She fought hard to keep breathing.

The door opened. Dr. Ing glided in on rubber-soled shoes. "Hello, folks. I can feel a hot summer ahead, can't you?"

All Ruth could feel was the gathering winds of a bitter winter. "Is the baby okay?"

Dr. Ing peered at the screen as he passed the wand from side to side. His eyes widened almost imperceptibly. He put the wand down and slid off his rubber gloves. "I can't believe we missed it."

His look was compassionate, but she could not see it clearly through her tears.

11

June afternoons in Finny would be perfect, Jack thought, if people would just take a break from sin and let the police have some time off. He sipped coffee from a travel mug and appreciated the brilliant sunlight as he drove toward Mrs. Hodges's house. Already since the butterfly tea ended, he'd corralled a menacing dog and discouraged a resident from building an eight-foot brick wall to keep nosy neighbors at bay.

His eyes wandered to the red tissue-paper flower that festooned the rearview mirror, Bobby's little joke. He wondered again why he couldn't say those three words she needed to hear. *Why is that so infernally hard for you, Jack? Let go of Lacey. She's dead, and she would have wanted you and Paul to move on.*

His head told him it was true, but his heart, or his conscience, would not sign on. So much for mind over matter. "God, help me, please. I'm making a mess of things down here." His prayer was cut short as he pulled up to Mrs. Hodges's cottage.

Alva met him at the front drive. His white hair stuck up from his scalp like fluffy icebergs. "It's a heinous crime, a traverstine of justice. They coulda been lying in wait. I coulda been murdered in my sleep or maybe tied up and smuggled to Barbados to work as a slave."

Jack held up a calming hand. "Let's just slow down here, Alva. What's the problem?"

"I done been burgled. Someone busted into my room

and went through my stuff."

"What was taken?"

"Nothin'. But that ain't the point."

Mrs. Hodges lumbered over, her round faced etched with concern. "Good afternoon, Jack. Come in for some cookies. I just took some out of the oven. Alva, would you go ahead and put some napkins on the table?"

With a grumble, the old man shuffled off.

She took Jack's arm as they headed into the house. "I thought Alva was just off on one of his tangents, but this time I think he's right."

Jack raised an eyebrow. "You think someone broke in?"

She nodded, setting her jowls wobbling. "They tried to, anyway. Come and have a look."

Jack forced himself to walk past the pan of still warm cookies in the kitchen, the aroma making his mouth water. Mrs. Hodges escorted them into Alva's room, a small whitewashed space that looked out on her prodigious vegetable garden, jammed with clusters of tomatoes just beginning to show color, and several zucchini plants decorated with showy yellow blossoms.

Alva scuttled by them and sat on his tidy bed, arms folded.

Jack noted a small wooden writing desk stacked with newspaper clippings and comic books. A crate at the foot of the bed held the rusty can opener and a hodgepodge of other dubious treasures.

"So, er, how do you know someone's been in here, Alva?"

Alva glared at the detective. "It's obvious, ain't it? Them books on my shelf been moved, and the dust under the bed's been stirred around."

Mrs. Hodges pinked. "I promised Alva when he came to live here that I wouldn't intrude on his privacy so the cleaning is up to him." She fanned her cheeks with a hand. "I can tell you there's no dust under any of the other beds in this house."

"Right." Jack peeked under the bed frame and scrutinized the bookshelf. "Alva, are you sure you didn't, uh, just look at some books and maybe forget you'd done it? Or maybe Mr. Hodges—" His voice trailed off at the ire kindling in the old man's eyes.

"Number first, I ain't prone to forgetting things, and number second, I ain't touched one of them books in all the years I done lived here."

Mrs. Hodges nodded. "He prefers comic books. And Mr. Hodges is out of town on a fishing trip. He doesn't go into Alva's room anyway."

Jack went outside to peer at the window that was open halfway. Alva trotted along at his heels. There was no sign of a forced entry. "Did you have it locked?"

Alva snorted. "Locked? What fer?"

Jack sighed. Mrs. Hodges pointed to the ground. There was no imprint of a foot, but she directed his attention to an overturned pot, pressed down into the earth.

"Someone needed a boost. That pot was right side up yesterday, with a new pepper plant in it."

Jack continued to scan the ground and windowsill for any telltale marks. "The guy or gal was careful anyway. What time do you guess they had access?"

Alva spoke up. "They came when I was out digging for treasure, I'll bet. I was gone from about seven to ten thirty. Then I spent the night at Petey's cuz it was Boy Scout camping night, so I didn't notice it until just now when I got back from walkin' Ruth to the jewelry store."

Mrs. Hodges nodded. "I didn't notice it either, but late night seems most likely. I was at a F.L.O.P meeting until around then. I know it definitely happened before eleven."

"Why?"

"I finished up watching the shopping network about then and let him into the garden."

"Who?"

"Pedro."

Jack couldn't restrain a nervous glance over his shoulder.

"It's okay." She patted the detective on the arm. "Pedro only has access to the yard during the night. He's in Mr. Peterman's field during the day doing weed control. Otherwise that goat would have mowed down any trespasser and chewed him into little bits."

Alva nodded, rubbing his knee thoughtfully. "I still got a piece missing from the last time Pedro waylaid me on my trip to the mail box."

Jack smiled. "Everyone who has ever met that goat has lost a part or two. It couldn't have been Pedro that upended the pot and ruined your pepper?"

Mrs. Hodges shook her head. "Pedro can't stand peppers."

Alva cackled. "Human flesh is more to his taste."

Jack nodded. "You're sure there's nothing missing?"

Alva shook his head. "Nah. Just some stuff moved around, kinda." His shaggy eyebrows drew together. "If I hadn'ta hidden my treasures, the burglar would have made off with a fortune."

Jack followed Mrs. Hodges and Alva into the kitchen. "What treasures are we talking about here, Alva?"

Alva settled himself into a chair and tucked a checked napkin around his neck. His voice dropped to a whisper.

"My jar of glass marbles is over at Bubby Dean's place. They'd be after that fer sure. And Ruth's got my baloney shell and a box of old coins I found on the beach. My collection of newspaper clippings is hidden in the fake potted plant at the library, but Big Foots don't know it. Good thing I spread 'em out, otherwise I'da lost it all."

Jack held up his coffee cup for Mrs. Hodges to fill. "Definitely a good thing. Has anyone been interested in your treasures lately? Asking questions, things like that?"

Alva jammed a cookie in his mouth, chewing carefully. "Nah, but I been pretty busy keeping track of Ruth and all. I'm her ninny, uh, nanny."

Jack and Mrs. Hodges exchanged a smile as the lady filled Jack's plate.

"Ya know," Alva said, eyes rolling around. "If I'da been home when he busted in, I might be dead now. He mighta conked me over the head and I'd be too dead to be eatin' these cookies now."

"Is anything disturbed in the rest of the house?" Jack tasted the gooey chocolate chip cookie. He would never take handouts or kickbacks, but it would be a sin to refuse a neighborly offer, especially from Mrs. Hodges, the best cook in the county.

"No, nothing else. I'm glad Mr. Hodges is going to be home today. I never would have thought someone would break into our house." She sat heavily in the chair, causing the floor to tremble. "Then again, I never would have thought someone would murder that poor cameraman, either."

Alva took a gulp of coffee. "Never say never."

Jack drove Alva to the police station so he could give a statement. It wasn't strictly necessary, as Jack could take one just as well from the cottage, but Alva was not going to be cheated out of his experience. The old man made sure to fill his pockets with change to use the station's vending machine.

"Best M&M's in Finny in yer machine," he said. "It's on account of the patina of terror that paints this place. The air is plumb filled with the aura of desperation from all of these hardened criminal types."

Jack raised an eyebrow. "Have you been watching a lot of television lately?"

He nodded. "*Masterpiece Theater*. Oh, just looky there. A desperate citizen, right in front of our noses." He made straight for Maude, who sat on a chair in the reception area with her ankle cast propped on a chair.

"Hey, Maude. Whatcha doin?"

She looked up from the book she was reading. "Not that it's any of your business, but I'm here to ask Jack to execute an investigation."

Jack forced himself to ask. "What kind of investigation?"

"I think we should check into Ellen's past, see what sins she has buried under that self-righteous facade. The more I think about it, the more convinced I am that she's not who she says she is." Her black eyes gleamed in her tiny face.

"We don't investigate citizens unless there's a good reason, Maude. Now if you'll excuse me, I've got to go."

Maude shot to her feet. "There is a good reason. She's poking around in other people's business all the time, as if she was collecting information or spying."

Alva laughed. "Sounds just like you, Maude."

She shot him a look of pure acid. "Stay out of it, you old goat."

Alva folded his scrawny arms. "It's clear as icicles that yer jealous cuz Ellen is tryin' to get her hooks into that dentist fella."

Maude colored. "Oh, fiddlesticks. That's ridiculous."

"I ain't thinkin' so."

She snorted. "You don't waste any time thinking, do you?"

A sly look crossed Alva's face. "I'm all wet, huh? Then I guess you ain't interested in what the doctor was buyin' at the jewelry store 'round lunchtime today. A real pretty thing, he bought, a romantic type thing."

Jack barely suppressed a smile at the change on Maude's face. Hooked like a trout, he thought.

"I'm not interested, no." She grabbed her purse and took a step to the door. "But Ellen probably already knows because she's a bigger snoop than you."

Alva chuckled. "Maybe. Or maybe she knows because he done gave the gold heart locket to her. Wouldn't that be something?"

Maude's expression kindled a surge of guilt in Jack. There was a sadness and vulnerability there that he had never seen before. For the first time he realized how lonely it might be for Maude. *Forgive me, Lord, for judging.* He summoned the words of Romans 14:10 in his mind. *You, then, why do you judge your brother? Or why do you look down on your brother? For we will all stand before God's judgment seat.* And the Lord already knew he had plenty to answer for. "Maybe we can talk later, Maude, after I'm done with Alva."

She waved a hand at him as she stumped away. "You're wasting your time with that geezer. He won't help you catch anything but a cold."

Maude left and Alva toddled away to stock up on candy. Jack said a hello to Nate and Mary, who were both keeping company in the coffee room until Maude left.

Nate looked around Jack's shoulder. "Is it safe to come out now?"

"Yes. Maude's gone. Can you take Alva's statement?"

"I'll do it." Before Mary cleared the door she stopped. "Oh, I almost forgot to tell you something I found out about our cameraman."

"The dead one or the living one?"

"Reggie, not Ethan. He's got a local connection."

Jack waited for her to finish.

"He got busted for some petty theft stuff along with a kid named Eddie Seevers."

Jack's brow furrowed. "Okay. What's the connection?"

"Eddie Seevers was Roxie Trotter's son."

"Was?"

"Drug overdose five years ago."

Nate tapped his mustache. "Five years? Isn't that about the time Roxie came to Finny?"

Jack sighed. "I guess I'm on my way to visit Ms. Trotter, then." He headed back out to the car. *But I can spare a few minutes to stop by Monk's for a cup of coffee,* he thought, crossing his fingers that a certain lady would be there to pour it for him.

⁓

Bobby was there, but she was up to her elbows in dough. Even worse, Jack noticed, she was deep in conversation with Ethan Ping. He tried to tamp down the irritation that flared in his gut as he took his coffee to a table. Sandra Marconi sat nearby, soaking in the sunshine that poured through the glass window.

She gazed out at the glittering expanse of ocean that was visible down slope from the coffee shop.

"Hello, Ms. Marconi. How goes the filming?"

She jumped, almost spilling her tea. "Filming? Oh, er, fine. Thanks for asking."

"Are you finding it hard to work without your official cameraman?"

"No. Ethan is great with a camera."

"How is he with salvage work?"

She blinked. "What?"

"Underwater salvage, for historical artifacts and such."

"I, uh, I don't know. We've never done that before. Why do you ask?"

He let the silence linger for a moment. "Reggie did some questionable recovery work, so I wondered if Ethan was in on it."

She blanched. "No. He's here to direct a film for our project, that's all. I've got to go." She hopped out of her seat and went to the door.

Darting a quick look in Jack's direction, Ethan said

good-bye to Bobby and followed Sandra out.

Jack approached the counter. Before he could speak, Bobby shot him a look.

"Scaring away our customers, Detective?"

"Not at all, just having a friendly conversation, like you were with him."

She opened her mouth to reply when the phone rang. "Monk's Coffee and Catering." After a second her eyes widened. "Okay. Okay, yes, I'll come over right now. Are you at home? Okay, I'll close up here this minute." She stood with the phone dangling from her fingers.

Jack took the receiver gently and hung it up. "What is it, Bobby? What's wrong?"

"That was Uncle Monk. They just met with the doctor. I need to go."

Monk went to find Ruth a drink of water while she pulled her clothes on with shaking fingers. She made it to the hallway and slid into a chair, chin on hands, and let the cool air bathe her heated face.

Her insides felt like the tiny seeds of a dandelion, blown in all directions by a careless wind.

"Hello, Ruth."

She looked up to find Roxie, emerging from a room a few doors down.

"Hi, Roxie." Her voice trembled only a little.

Roxie pulled on her knit cap and looked at Ruth for a minute, before sinking into a chair next to her. "Looks like you're having a bad day."

"I—" Ruth clamped her mouth shut to avoid bursting into tears.

Roxie sighed. "I've been there."

Ruth noticed a square of white tape on the woman's arm. She swallowed hard. "Are you okay?"

"Sure, sure. I get regular blood tests because my kidney is failing."

Ruth was temporarily jerked from her malaise. "Oh, I'm so sorry to hear that."

"It's okay. I've gotten used to the idea. Normally I go to a hospital in San Francisco. They've got a specialist there who is determined to keep me alive, in spite of all the given facts." She fingered the tape. "I had an appointment in the city yesterday. Saw Dr. Soloski there. I don't know what his problem is, but our paths cross a lot at that hospital."

Ruth pressed the balled-up tissue to her nose again.

Roxie gave her a sidelong look. "Say, if you'd rather be alone. . ."

"No, no. I—I've just had a shock, is all. It's—it's. . . twins." Saying the words aloud almost sent her into a shower of tears again.

"Twins?" Roxie smiled. "Oh, boy. Double blessing, huh?"

"I know that's what I should be feeling. Twins are a miracle, an amazing special gift times two. I should be on my knees thanking God, but all I can think of is, how will I cope?"

The words gathered momentum and flew out in a steady stream. "I'm going to be forty-nine, and I didn't do a good job the first time I had a child. I spoiled him, sheltered him from disappointments so he never learned how to deal with them. And now—" She swallowed a tide of rising panic.

"Not me," Roxie said. "I was a perfect mother. I was patient, but firm. I had rules and plenty of structure with time left over for fun. As both the mother and dad I was great, even if I do say so." She handed Ruth another tissue. "You know what? My son turned out to be a screw-up, and eventually his choices got the better of him and they are getting the better of me an inch at a time. He couldn't keep away from trouble and it killed him, just like it killed Reggie."

Ruth straightened, wondering at the connection between Roxie's son and the dead cameraman.

Roxie gazed at the worn tiles on the floor. "It killed me, too, really, only my death is taking awhile longer." She shook her head. "Anyway, the thing is, Ruth, I couldn't have loved him more if he'd turned out to be the president of the United States instead of a deadbeat."

She stood. "Funny, isn't it? It doesn't really matter who they are or what they decide to be, or even how many in the batch. Mothers love their children in spite of everything. Where did we learn how to do that, I wonder?"

Roxie patted Ruth on the shoulder and left, as Monk arrived, puffing, with a bottle of water.

⁓

They walked back to the cottage in relative silence. Monk's expression changed alternately from wonder to abject fear. Several times he started to speak but sputtered into silence. He settled for gripping her hand firmly in his, as if she might fly away if he let go.

She couldn't keep her mind on any practical thought. It kept spinning back to the incredible truth: twins. The writhing bundle of kicks and pokes was the project of two babies. Two. She had to rest for a minute to stop the spinning in her head.

They'd made it several blocks when Alva caught up with them. "Oh, sakes," he said, wringing his cap between his hands. "I was at the hospital getting me some of that free coffee when I done heard the news." He panted and pressed a hand over his heart. "Don't let it worry you none. Even if it comes out with scales and a tail we'll love it, you'll see."

Monk gaped at him. "What are you talking about?"

"The baby. I heard it's gonna have fins, but don't you pay it no mind. My cousin Swannie had webbed toes and we didn't respect her none the less. Besides she was an expert at the swimmin' pool. We'll love the little bun in Ruth's oven, fins or no fins."

Ruth felt a swell of laughter building. She managed a quick, "Twins, not fins," before she started to laugh.

Alva blinked. "Twins? Ain't that what they call a pair?" He pointed to her stomach. "Two of them in that compartment?"

She nodded, giggles escaping like spurts of steam. Monk began to guffaw, too, until all three of them roared with laughter.

Alva wiped his eyes. "Well, that's a relief, ain't it? I'll just go back to the hospital and tell 'em they made an error. Whew. I thought we was goin' to have to keep it in an aquarium."

Ruth and Monk got the hysterical laughter out of their systems by the time they made it home. Bobby and Jack were waiting on the front step when they arrived. Both shot to their feet and stood awkwardly. Then Bobby wrapped Ruth in an enormous hug, and Jack pumped Monk's hand vigorously before they all entered the sitting room.

"I can't believe it," Jack said. "Twins. Amazing."

"My sentiments exactly." Monk's wide face was still pale. "I don't believe there's a propensity for doubles in either of our families that we know of."

Ruth took the steaming cup of tea gratefully from Bobby's hand.

"Aunt Ruth, is everything. . .all right with the babies?"

She inhaled the herbal steam for a moment, willing it to sooth her jangled nerves. "Yes, they are perfectly fine, as far as Dr. Ing can tell. One is a little small, but not abnormally so." She read the question on Bobby's face. "We decided not to know the gender."

Jack smiled. "Going for the surprise finish. I like it."

Monk smiled back. "It seems like we've had a big enough surprise for one day."

The look Monk gave Ruth was so tender it made her want to start crying again. Instead she changed the subject. "Jack, how is the investigation going?"

"Nowhere fast. There is some question about the folks funding this historical project." He shot Bobby a look. "And Reggie was a man who lived on the fringes, that's for sure."

Ruth recalled the strange comment from Roxie. "Have you, er, found out if Reggie was working with anyone besides the college people?"

Jack gave her a sharp look. "Why?"

"Oh, just something Roxie said about her son, comparing him to Reggie. It just struck me as odd."

"Odd for sure. Her son, Eddie Seevers, was in trouble on and off. Some of it with Reggie. Small time, mostly."

"Jack, what happened to Eddie?"

"He died. Lost a kidney as a complication from drug use, and his mother gave him one of hers. Died of an OD."

Ruth sighed. The pain must be unbearable for poor Roxie. "At least she can breathe easy knowing Eddie wasn't responsible for what happened to Reggie."

"He's in the clear for sure." Jack jammed his hands into his pockets.

"You sound doubtful," Monk said.

Bobby laughed. "I think he's always a little doubtful."

"It's just a question of who knew whom. Eddie knew

Reggie before the guy was strangled. So did Roxie, and she never mentioned it to me. That's a pretty big omission."

Monk nodded in agreement. "Yes, can't exactly blame that on forgetfulness. Any luck tracing that knot?"

Jack shook his head. "No."

In spite of the shiver in the pit of her stomach, Ruth could not suppress a yawn. "I'm so sorry. This day is catching up with me."

Jack and Bobby gave her a hug, and Bobby whispered in her ear, "It's going to be okay, Aunt Ruth. We'll be here with you every step of the way."

Too overcome with emotion to speak, Ruth squeezed her hand.

The house settled into quiet. Monk busied himself wiping down the kitchen counters, taking out the trash, and dusting until Ruth couldn't stand it anymore. "Monk. Stop. Please just stop and tell me this is going to be okay."

He stood frozen for a moment. Then he came over to the sofa where she sat and knelt next to her. "Ruthy, I'll be perfectly honest and tell you the idea of having a pair of babies gave me a turn. To think, two to hold and juggle around, and the bills—" His gaze became unfocused.

Her eyes started to fill. "I know. I can't believe it. At our age. What are we going to do?"

He blinked. "Do? We should take action to prepare."

"How do you prepare for this exactly?"

"We're going to start by making a list right now." He fetched a pencil and began writing. "Two cribs for sure." His brow crinkled. "Is it two cribs, Ruth? Or do you just kind of stack them in one?"

She gave him a look of complete exasperation. "I have no idea."

"Okay. I'll put a question mark next to that one. Two car seats and sets of bottles. How about strollers? Do they make two-seaters, or do you get singles and strap a couple of them together?"

She squeezed her eyes shut. "Lord, help us. We are in double trouble."

Monk grabbed his keys and gave her a peck on the cheek. "I better go buy a book about this twin stuff. I'll be back soon."

~~~

Ruth spent the evening fluttering from one thing to the next like a hyperactive bee, accomplishing nothing of consequence. She heard Bryce come home after eight, hair tousled from time spent at the beach. Monk was still gone, trying to catch up on the catering work he'd fallen behind on due to their doctor's appointment. She lay in the bed, too tired even to get up and see if her son needed anything. The slam of his bedroom door told her he was still brooding about things. She knew firsthand how difficult it was to disentangle two lives. Roslyn was removing herself from Bryce's life as effectively as Phillip's death had removed him from hers. She'd never thought of divorce in that light before. It was like a death, in a way.

Divorce. The word sent a shudder through her spine. What would she do if Monk left? How would she cope without him? Alone, with two babies. What if the strain of having an instant houseful sent him over the edge?

Desperate to take her mind off the future, she grabbed the notebook from the bed stand and flipped it open. Indigo's life was much more fun to think about than her own at the moment.

The spring has been a mild one, praise God. The twisted pear tree outside my tent has a promising collection of buds. I have tagged each blossom with the name of a miner who will pay two dollars and fifty cents for the chance to have his own pear when summer comes. It makes Hui laugh to see the paper tags dancing in the wind, festooning the branches like dozens of kites.

In the afternoons, sometimes, if the sun is shining, we hunt for mushrooms. Hui knows which ones can be eaten and he has shown me how to dry them along with some seaweed he collected. I do not know what we will concoct with these exotic ingredients, but it eases my mind to know that we have started to collect some bits of food against the harsher winter weather which will come.

Hui has shown me something that may help us save enough to buy a little shop someday. He told me about something called a Hangtown Fry. It was hard to understand him at first, but I surmised it to be a type of dish made of an egg scramble with bacon and oysters mixed in. They call it egg foo yung in his country, but here it is a delicacy. The men are quite willing to pay two dollars a plate for it. Two dollars! Hui swims like a minnow, so he dives along the edge of the surf and pries the oysters from the bottom. If he cannot reach the oysters, we use abalone instead and the men seem just as happy. Though it terrifies me to watch his dark head disappear under the water, he is thrilled beyond measure when he hands over the lumpy oysters and whatever abalone he can find.

We pry them open and he crushes the shells to add to the glittering walkway that leads from our tent to the beach. Twice now he has even found a pearl. They are irregularly shaped and oddly colored so there is no sense to sell them. It brings me greater joy to see how he likes to keep them in his pocket, taking them out now and then when the men aren't around to see them shine in the sun.

Hui sees treasure in things that other people take for rubbish. To think that Señor Orson worked so hard for his treasure and lost his life in the process while we reap riches tossed up from the ocean straight from the fingers of God.

I have heard that we are lucky to have so many oysters and abalone to make our Hangtown Fry. The miners in areas farther south have stripped all the good sized beds. All the better for us as the rare traveler to these parts will pay handsomely for his supper, too.

Ruth closed the notebook when the phone rang.
"Hello, Mrs. Budge?"
"Yes, hi, Sandra."
"Hi. Um, I was wondering if you could tell me if there's a convenience store anywhere close by? Everything

seems closed up tight."

She checked the clock to find it was almost nine. "That's Finny for you. We roll up the sidewalks at six o'clock. You'd have to drive to the next town for a convenience store open at this hour. Is there something I can help you with?"

"Oh, uh, no, not really. I just needed some disinfectant and gauze."

"Are you hurt?"

"No, no. Ethan is scraped a little."

"Scraped? What happened?"

"We were out walking, and he fell and cut himself on some metal."

"Really? Does he need stitches? There's a hospital right off Whist Street. They can fix him up there."

"Ethan is kind of private. He doesn't want to make a big deal out of it. Never mind, Ruth. It's not that important."

"Why don't you come over here? I've got bandages and gauze. Please. I'd be happy to help out."

Sandra hesitantly agreed. Ruth threw on some clothes. When Sandra arrived fifteen minutes later, her cheeks were pink from the walk.

Ruth looked around. "You didn't bring Ethan with you?"

"Ah, no. I told you he's really private. I'll just take the supplies back over and clean him up."

"Are you sure he isn't going to need some stitches?"

"No, no. He's fine."

Bryce came into the kitchen and greeted them. Ruth explained the situation.

"Who would think taking a walk was so hazardous?" Sandra laughed nervously.

"What did he cut himself on?"

Sandra shrugged. "A drainpipe, I think. Sticking up from the ground. Can you believe it?" She grabbed the supplies and thanked Ruth again before she scurried out the door.

Bryce frowned. "You know, Mom, an hour ago I was walking down by the cliffs."

She waited for him to continue.

"Funny thing, but I saw two people suiting up for a dive."

"A dive? At night? Who were they?"

"I couldn't see the guy real well, but I recognized the girl all right."

Her own face pulled into a puzzled frown. "Sandra Marconi?"

"Uh-huh, and I sure never heard of anyone taking a walk wearing a wet suit."

13

Ruth spent Saturday in a blur of activity. She felt the urgent need to cook, clean, garden, whatever would help her prepare her mind and house for the arrival of the babies. She didn't remember eating, or the sporadic visits from her husband. There was only work and the eventual collapse into bed at an insanely early hour.

She woke the next morning in a mass of twisted sheets, her body covered with cold sweat. Her eyes flew open. Twins. It hadn't been a dream. She clamped her lids shut and tried to take a couple of deep breaths. When she opened them again, the frightening fact remained: She was still pregnant with not one baby but two.

How did one even birth two babies, let alone raise them? Maybe Monk had the right idea. She should start reading every book she could on this wild and scary topic. *No,* she thought firmly. With Bryce she'd read every book ever penned on the subject, and all that did was make her feel inferior. She was going to let God handle things this time and hope it all turned out better. What did God do with His children? He loved them unconditionally. He did not spare them from disappointment and sorrow, but He guided them through the pain. She thought about Roxie.

Mothers love their children in spite of everything. Where did we learn how to do that, I wonder? Ruth knew. There was only one model of perfect love.

She felt a surge of confidence. "I can do this," she said

aloud. "I can raise two babies."

Climbing out of bed, she enjoyed the fleeting moment of peace. Then she went into the bathroom and threw up.

On her way to the kitchen, an iridescent flutter of color caught her eye. It was Alva's abalone shell, winking against the flood of morning light. She picked it up, thinking of Indigo and her glittering path of crushed oysters and abalone. The thought pleased her. Treasures tossed up from the fingers of God. Absently she stowed the shell into her purse to return it to Alva before the hapless Carson showed up to wreak more havoc on the house.

After a breakfast of dry toast and weak tea she composed herself enough to make it to church, where she slid into the seat Monk saved for her. "How are things at the restaurant?" she whispered in his ear.

"Fine, just fine." His eyes rolled in thought. "Say, Ruth, do you think we ought to consider having a bathroom added onto the house? I mean, aren't we going to need two of everything? Maybe we could squeeze in double sinks, but they'll just have to share a shower. No way we can fit in two of those."

The look she gave him must have blasted the idea away because he cleared his throat and patted her hand. "Um, never mind. We'll talk about that later."

The news had already spread throughout the congregation. Even Pastor Henny exclaimed over the miracle from his spot at the podium. The attendees cheered for Ruth and Monk as if they were rooting for a basketball team. Ruth's face flushed, and she tried to sneak out after the service.

She was waylaid by people offering their best wishes

and folks reaching out to touch her stomach. Feeling more like a parade float than a parishioner, she finally made it to the parking lot. Monk kissed her and offered to drive her home before opening the shop.

"No thanks. I could use a walk to clear my head." Then she started to giggle.

"What's so funny?"

"I was just thinking it's a good thing Alva didn't persuade everyone the babies were going to come out with fins."

He chuckled as he drove away.

Ruth strolled along the tree-lined sidewalk, oblivious to the clumps of rhododendron that provided a shelter for dozens of small birds. Her thoughts ran in anxious circles. Twins. How many bottles would she need for two babies? Would their car be big enough for a pair of car seats? High chairs! They only had the old wooden one of Bryce's. Did they make double seater high chairs now?

She groaned. "I'm beginning to sound like Monk." To avoid driving herself completely crazy, Ruth turned her energy to Indigo's writing. One line in particular danced in her head. *Señor Orson worked so hard for his treasure and lost his life in the process.* What could the treasure be? It must have been some valuable treasure indeed that Orson was willing to book passage on an overloaded coal ship instead of waiting for a proper steamer.

Curiosity drove her to the library, with only a quick stop to snack on the ever-present crackers she carried in her purse. Sundays were the best day to visit the library, as Ellen wouldn't be in until afternoon, leaving more genial volunteers to run the place in her absence.

Ruth sat at the computer, removing the abalone shell

from her purse when it poked her in the side, and did an Internet search on lost treasure. She found several entries about rock bands she'd never heard of, a perfume guaranteed to "turn the wearer into the queen of her destiny," and many articles about shipwrecks. With a sigh she turned her focus to Indigo's more practical treasure, typing in *Hangtown Fry*. The old computer was still stuck in think mode when a voice made her jump.

"As you can see, I run a tight ship here. No book out of place, no lights on unnecessarily. Every bit of paper recycled, and ink cartridges as well." Ellen stopped when she saw Ruth at the computer. "What are you doing here on a Sunday?"

A weary-looking Dr. Soloski stood just behind her, still wearing his suit from church. "Hello, Mrs. Budge."

"Hello, folks. I didn't expect to see you today, Ellen. I was just doing a little research."

Ellen fisted a hand on her hip. "I see. And what is the topic du jour? Anything you need help with?" She snatched up the shell. "What's this?"

Ruth felt suddenly embarrassed. "It's Alva's shell."

The doctor smiled. "Ah. I thought it looked familiar."

Ellen gave a ferocious snort. "You've seen one shell, you've seen them all." Her eyes swiveled back to Dr. Soloski.

He looked at Ruth as though he were a drowning man asking for a life preserver.

Ruth began to babble. "Oh, well, this shell is really nice. It's smaller than the other abalone, and it doesn't weigh very much." She decided to change the topic. "Dr. Soloski, Roxie said she saw you at the hospital in San Francisco. I hope everything is all right."

His eyebrows shot up. "Oh, yes. Everything is fine, thank you for asking. I go there weekly to visit Jane."

Ellen's eyes narrowed. "Jane?"

"My sister. She's been disabled since birth. I became her caretaker when my mother died five years ago. I brought her a locket."

"Ohhh." Ellen patted his shoulder, relief shining across her face. "Such a good son. Jane is so lucky to have a brother like you." She returned her attention to Ruth. "You enjoy your research," she said, taking Dr. Soloski by the arm. "I'm sure you'll be an expert in no time. Just remember, you don't get pearls from abalone." She laughed again, the sound echoing through the quiet library.

Dr. Soloski shot her a rueful look as he was dragged away.

The computer finally finished its cyber cogitation and the screen popped up with several articles on the infamous Hangtown Fry. True to Indigo's description, the dish was indeed a scramble of eggs, bacon, and oysters. One tale about the recipe attributed it to a condemned man who requested the dish for his last meal, figuring the difficulty in acquiring the rare ingredients would provide him a stay of execution.

"I wonder if it worked for him," Ruth muttered. Sadly, she noted, the shellfish were such a hit, many of the oyster beds were depleted by 1851. Abalone suffered the same fate. Another case where humans had disrupted God's careful balance.

A kick from her belly button region spurred her to turn off the computer, pack up Alva's shell, and head to the stacks. She grabbed a couple of books on Pacific Coast ocean life and one about famous shipwrecks before she sat down to read. Settled in the sunny corner on a padded chair, Ruth made it all the way to page two before she fell asleep.

She awoke an hour later with just enough time to scurry home, unload the bulky shell from her purse, grab the relevant pages from Indigo's life story, and make it to the beach for rehearsal. As she hurried up the path to the film site, Maude waved from her position at the head of a half dozen gray-haired ladies. Ruth tried to dodge in the other direction, but it was no use.

"And this is Ruth Budge. She's a feature actor in the project." Maude beamed. "As you can see, she's expecting. Twins, can you believe it? At her age. Though she's sick all the time and obviously bloated, she shows up nonetheless. She's an inspiration to us all. Ruth, won't you share a few words with my tour group?"

Ruth wanted to share a few choice words all right, but she managed to control her temper. "It's been a very interesting project. Thanks so much for coming." She tried to edge by a disappointed-looking Maude.

"Oh, come now," Maude said. "No time for modesty. Ruth is also somewhat of a sleuth. I'm sure you heard about the murder at the Fog Festival? The balloon crash?"

The gaggle of women nodded, wide-eyed.

"Well, Ruth here was the one who solved the crime. With plenty of help, of course, not a little of which came from yours truly. Isn't that right, Ruth?"

She gave Maude a dark look. "I'd rather not relive it, thank you."

"And then there is the body of Reggie the cameraman

tossed up on our gravelly shore only days ago. The police are very close lipped but there's no doubt it's"—Maude dropped her voice to a whisper—"murder."

The word elicited gasps from the ladies.

"And once again here is our Ruth Budge, deep in the thick of it. How does that make you feel, Ruth?"

She sighed. "The only thing I feel at the moment is queasy. Enjoy your visit." She dodged around Maude and headed to Ethan and Sandra, who sat at a card table going over some papers. "Who knew you'd have tour groups coming to see your project before it was even finished?"

Ethan sniffed. "Who indeed? I told them they had to stay back at the edge of the grassy area and so far they're following orders."

He wore long pants so Ruth could not see where he had been injured. "Ethan, are you okay? Sandra told me you cut yourself last night."

He nodded at her. "Yes, I'm fine. Thanks for asking."

"Great." She thought out her words before she dropped them. "You know, my son was out for a jog last night, and he saw you two ready to dive. Were you doing some photography for the project?"

Ethan's eyes widened and Sandra's mouth fell open. "No," he said firmly. "We weren't diving. Your son must have been mistaken."

"Hmm. Night diving is such a bad idea, nobody around here would try such a thing. Bryce was pretty convinced it was you two."

His dark eyes bored into hers. "Of course it wasn't us. Diving at night is ludicrous, as we learned the hard way with Reggie. Must have been some tourists or something."

He shuffled his papers and smiled at her. "Let's get to work, shall we? We wouldn't want to disappoint our tour group." He gestured to the gaggle of women who smiled and waved at him.

Sandra walked her over to the shelter of some eucalyptus where they had erected a shack to represent Indigo's hideaway. She helped Ruth slip on a blousy tunic and rough boots. Ruth noticed Sandy's hands shaking. "So it really wasn't you and Ethan diving last night?"

Sandra jerked as if she'd been slapped. "No, no. Just what he said, we were walking. It's nice here for walking." She fiddled with the tie on Ruth's tunic. "A lovely town, even at night."

Ruth considered. "You know I've been reading my script and it seems Señor Orson had some kind of treasure on board the *Triton* when it went down." Ruth eyed her closely.

Sandra blinked several times. "Treasure? Oh yes, we caught that reference. Here's your hat."

"What do you think it was?"

"What?"

"Señor Orson's treasure. What do you think it was?"

Sandra attempted a smile. "Beats me. Could be figurative. Maybe he was referring to his wife. It could have been an heirloom that meant something only to him. You know what they say, one man's trash is another man's treasure. I'll go tell Ethan you're ready."

As Ruth waited for Sandra to return, she watched the afternoon sun catch bits of metallic sparkle in the crushed rock under her feet. She tried to picture the spot as it had looked in the 1800s, with the glittering pathway of broken oyster shells. Sandra was right, one man's trash was another man's treasure, but she was more and more convinced that Sandra and Ethan were in search of something more precious than a historical reenactment. She resolved to keep her ears open for more information.

They worked through the scene several times. At the end of the session, Sandra helped her remove the costume. "Good work today, Mrs. Budge. We should be able to wrap up in the next few days."

"Really? So soon?"

"Yes. We've decided to abridge the project a little." She fingered the costume's worn material. "Actually, we should probably get the script back from you so we can go over it and see if there's anything we missed."

"Don't you have a copy?"

"Oh, well, sure we do, but we've made notes on both and it's just good practice to be thorough. Right?"

"Of course. I'll bring the whole thing back tomorrow."

"I'm going to be out later today. I'd be happy to come by and get it."

Ruth smiled sweetly. "No need, Sandra. I'll bring it tomorrow." *Right after I read every word of it.*

———

Ruth met Monk and Bryce that evening for dinner. She hadn't had time that afternoon to finish the script since Carson arrived to replace the ravaged sheetrock. Though he was a small man with a wild mop of curly black hair, he made more noise than a high school football team.

A knock at the door just after six made her jump,

but Monk only smiled. "Excellent. They really do deliver quick." A uniformed man stood on the doorway chomping on a wad of gum. He handed Monk a clipboard.

Monk scrawled his signature and the parade of packages began. A massive carton with a picture of two blissful babies sleeping side by side in a crib came first, followed by two car seats, two inflatable baby bathtubs, and a pair of bouncy seats.

Monk beamed as he arranged the wall of boxes in the middle of the sitting room. "Take a look at this, Ruthy. The bouncy seats vibrate. It's supposed to jiggle 'em around so they fall asleep. Quite an invention. Amazing, huh?"

"Sure, amazing," she answered weakly as the mountain of boxes grew.

Bryce lent a hand to carry in several unmarked cartons and an enormous package containing a changing table complete with a colorful clown mobile.

Ruth gasped. The pile of baby things grew along with the tension in her stomach. She felt closed in by a cardboard prison. "Where are we going to put all of this stuff?"

Monk whistled happily as he returned from the garage with a toolbox. "Don't worry, hon. I'll get it all assembled, and we'll put the nursery to rights."

Ruth stepped over a box boasting a set of teddy bears that made noises similar to a mother's heartbeat. If the thing was realistic, the heart would sound like a jackhammer right about now. "But, Monk, we haven't even painted the nursery yet. Carson hasn't finished the patching up yet. Don't you think we should do that first?"

That caused him to pause. "Oh. Well, no matter. We'll

store the gear in the garage until he's done. How's that?"

"I can help you paint," Bryce offered.

The room continued to close in on her until she could stand it no longer. "Fine, fine. I'm going to take the birds out for their walk. I'll be back soon."

Monk didn't look up from the pile of screws and washers and an ominous-looking set of directions. "Okay, honey. Be careful. I've got this under control, Bryce. You go on with your mother."

She got her coat and made sure there was a bag of Fritos in the pocket before she let herself out into the yards. The birds milled around, eager for their nightly stroll. Bryce joined her as she headed down the drive.

"Mind a little company?"

"Of course not." Truth be told, Ruth would have preferred to be alone with her dark thoughts. Her house, her life was being transformed into baby playland before her very eyes. She should be joyous, welcoming every tiny toy and tool. But she wasn't. God help her, she wasn't.

They walked in silence for a while, the only sound coming from the quiet scratch of the birds' feet on the earthy shoulder that ran next to the road. The sky was almost dark, the creeping cool of night whispering in as they strolled.

Bryce's phone rang, the sound harsh in the quiet of the evening. The conversation was short. "Yes. Yes, I'll look for it. Okay. Right." He hung up, his face a mask of rage. "That was Roslyn. She is faxing the papers for the sale of the house. Apparently we've got to make it snappy so she can start her new life with flower boy. I need to go meet with a lawyer."

Ruth sighed. "Where will you go after the house is sold?"

He shrugged.

The words came out straight from her heart before she had time to think better of them. "Maybe you should come out here." Seeing his face change, she regretted the comment as soon as she said it. *Meddling, Ruth, meddling.*

"Mom, that's just why I left," he snapped. "Don't tell me what to do. I don't like to have my life managed for me."

She felt like she'd been slapped. "I guess that wasn't my business. I apologize."

He didn't answer.

Suddenly her hurt changed to anger. "Bryce, what about your baby?"

"My baby?" His eyes shone in the gloom. "There is no baby. Roslyn miscarried, remember?"

"I know. And you're grieving about that, I can tell. So this baby, this life that you never even met, you felt something for, didn't you?"

He nodded. "Sure."

"So let yourself imagine for a minute, if you can, what you would feel for a child that has actually been born, Bryce. It's everything to you. It's your heart walking around outside your body and you try to keep it from getting hurt. I know I protected you too much. I managed you too much, but I did it because I love you, and I would think that creating a child of your own, you could understand that in some small way." Her voice quivered, her breath coming in pants. She clamped her lips tightly together.

He was quiet for a minute as they walked.

Now he will really be chomping at the bit to leave, she thought miserably.

Finally he spoke. "I guess you're right, Mom. I was

out of line. I—I'm sorry."

Her eyes filled inexplicably with tears. "Me, too, Bryce. I wish I hadn't tried to keep disappointment away so much. Maybe it would be easier for you now." She reached out her hand for his.

He squeezed her fingers. "I think it would still hurt just as much." He cleared his throat. "I've got to go to San Francisco to finalize the divorce."

How sad he looked. How unutterably sad. She was so overwhelmed by the swirl of emotion she did not hear it at first.

The roar of an engine coming from behind.

There was no time to escape.

The last thing she saw was the startled look in her son's eyes as the car bore down on them both.

14

Jack's ears were still ringing as he pulled up to the Budge cottage. Monk had bellowed into the phone that someone had tried to run down his wife. It didn't matter that Jack was off duty for the evening. Cops were never really off duty in a small town. Not that it made a speck of difference. The thought of Ruth being in the path of a hit-and-run driver was more than enough to send him back into cop mode.

"Thanks, God, for Louella," he whispered, as he had many times before. The woman was sent directly by the Lord, he was sure, to pull his bacon out of the fire on a regular basis. Nonetheless he hoped Paul wouldn't wake up and find out he was gone again.

He pulled on a windbreaker against the night, which was thick with clouds that screened the pale moonlight. Hints of an early summer storm hung in the air. His fist didn't quite make it to the door to knock before it was yanked open and Monk ushered him inside.

The big man looked completely unglued, face flushed, brow sweaty. "I'm glad you're here, Jack. I can't believe it. I should have been with her, not doodling around with the crib. To think what could have happened. I'd never forgive myself, never."

Jack gripped his arm. "Let's not play any blame games now, Monk. I need to know what happened."

Monk led him to Ruth, who sat on the sofa with a blanket on her lap and an untouched cup of tea on the coffee table, holding a gauze bandage to her elbow. "Hello, Jack."

"Hi, Ruth. I thought I'd be visiting you at the hospital. Are you sure you don't want to go get checked out?"

She raised her chin a fraction. "No. I've been through this already with Monk and Bryce. Bryce pulled me out of the way and I landed on top of him, poor guy. I only scraped my elbow. He took the brunt of it. I wouldn't be surprised if he had some broken ribs or something."

"Are you hurt?" Jack asked.

Bryce shrugged from where he stood next to the fireplace. "No. Like she said, I pulled her to the side and we both went over backward, but no harm done. The birds managed to get out of the way, too. We couldn't see who was driving."

"Do you think it was intentional?"

Ruth shook her head. "I'm sure it wasn't. It was dark, we were near a turn. The driver probably didn't even see us. We shouldn't have been walking late, but there are never really any cars on the road there that I've ever encountered."

Bryce looked at her but didn't say anything.

Jack caught his eye. "Is that what you think, Bryce?"

"No. I think it was deliberate. Whoever it was turned off their headlights as they accelerated and drove onto the shoulder on purpose. Sorry, Mom." He shot a look at his mother, who blanched.

"This is intolerable." Monk's face flushed even darker. "Who would do such a thing? To Ruth. To the babies." His hands balled into fists. "If I ever get my hands on the driver—"

"Leave that to us. We'll find out who did it. Any impression about the car make and model? Color?" He looked from Ruth to Bryce and back again.

"It was small," Ruth said. "That's about all I can say."

"I agree with Mom. Some sort of compact model, dark color, is about all I picked up. We were too busy trying to get out of the way to pay much attention."

Jack fiddled with his pencil as he looked at Bryce. "Have you had any problems since you came to Finny?"

"Me? No. I left my problems behind in Chicago."

Ruth gave Monk a smile as he pressed her hand. "Why do you ask?"

Bryce gave his mother a dark look. "He's wondering if the guy who tried to run us down tonight might have been after me."

The room fell into an uneasy silence.

"Who would want to run you down?" Ruth's voice had a slight quaver.

"I don't know, Mom, but in a way, I'd rather somebody was after me than you."

Ruth's cheeks pinked and she blinked hard. "This is crazy but, maybe, I mean I'm not sure or anything, but I wonder—"

Jack waited patiently.

"Well, I have this feeling the college people are up to something. Bryce saw them suiting up for a night dive but they denied it, said they were out walking. That's odd, isn't it? Of course, it certainly doesn't mean they would try to run either of us down. I'm sure they wouldn't do that. They just don't look like the kind of people who could be capable of such a thing."

Jack smiled. "That's why I like you, Ruth. You never seem to think people are capable of the terrible things they do."

Monk kissed Ruth on the forehead. "I like that about her, too."

"Okay." Jack sighed. "It's not much to go on, but maybe somebody else saw something. I'll check with the locals along that strip of road."

Monk stood with him and lowered his voice. "I am going to keep a close eye on her, Jack. I'll take some time off."

"Oh, no, you won't." Ruth put down the cup with a sharp clank. "You are not going to take time off to babysit me. I am perfectly fine. When I have to walk the birds, I'll take someone with me. Bryce, you'll go, won't you?"

He nodded. "Sure."

"And if he's not home, I'll take Alva."

Monk gave her a dubious look.

"Or Bobby," she added hastily.

"Nothing against your son or Bobby, Ruthy, but I think it would be better for me to stay with you."

Ruth stood awkwardly. "You need to work, Monk. Otherwise who will pay for all this?" She waved a hand at the mountain of boxes. "Besides, it will drive me crazy to have you hovering all the time, as much as I love you."

He huffed. "I still think—"

"Jack will look into this accident or whatever it was. Right, Jack?"

"Absolutely."

Monk put a hand on her shoulder. "But he may not have any luck, Ruthy. It's not going to be easy going, is it, Jack?"

"No, honestly it'll be another mountain to climb, but I'm used to that."

Bryce snapped his fingers. "A mountain to climb. That's

what I've been trying to remember."

They all stared at him.

He shook his head. "Don't know why I didn't come up with that earlier. I remembered where I saw Roxie's picture before."

Jack frowned. "Roxie Trotter?"

"Yeah. She used to live in Chicago. She was some sort of professional person, I think. I remember reading about her in the local paper because she was into mountain climbing. Made it to the top of Mt. McKinley in record time."

"Roxie was a professional?" Ruth's face crinkled in confusion, thinking about Roxie's attempt to sell shells to the jeweler. "She seems to have fallen on hard times."

"What are you thinking, Jack?" Monk said.

Jack replayed a few facts from Reggie's murder in his mind. "I was just thinking that mountain climbing is an interesting sport. It requires lots of specialized equipment." He zipped his jacket and said under his breath, "I wonder how good Ms. Trotter is at tying knots."

In the morning, Ms. Trotter seemed to be doing her best to tie Jack in knots. She sat, burrowed down in her ragged jacket, cap pulled to her eyebrows. The look she gave him was hostile at best. "Give it your best shot, Detective. Try to prove I killed Reggie. The guy probably drowned on his own, out doing a night dive. Stupid."

"He didn't drown."

She blinked, but her expression didn't change. "Not

my business how he died. I don't really care anyway."

Jack continued. "I'm not trying to prove you killed anyone. I just want to ask a few questions about your relationship with the deceased."

"I think the deceased was nothing but trouble. I didn't want him around my son, but since Eddie is dead, that was no longer an issue for me."

"Why didn't you want him around your son?"

"The same reason you wouldn't want him around yours. Because he hung out with the wrong people, people who drove nice cars and carried wads of cash without doing an honest day's work. Bad kind of people."

"Can you give me any names?"

"No. That was back in Chicago, and it was a lifetime ago."

Jack gave Nate an exasperated look.

Nate cleared his throat. "Say, Mrs. Trotter. I read somewhere you were a chiropractor. Still practicing? I've got a permanent kink in my neck."

She raised a thick eyebrow. "Does it look like I'm still practicing? I lost my license, as you well know."

"That's a bummer. What happened?"

"Again, I'm sure you already know every minuscule fact about my life, so why go into it?"

Jack fixed her with a look. "Because it would be helping us out. Think of it as doing your civic duty."

She glared at him for a moment. "I stole from some of my clients. Broke into their homes while they were on vacation. They didn't press charges so I avoided doing time, but I lost my license to practice."

"Really?" Nate tapped a pencil on the desk. "Seems like you had a pretty good client list. Business must have been good. Why jeopardize things by stealing?"

Her eyes glinted. "There's never enough money to go around, is there?"

Nate nodded. "I guess not. Wonder why the cops didn't charge you."

Roxie heaved a sigh. "They thought I was trying to cover for someone. Seems somebody saw me at the time of the last robbery in the grocery store. Isn't that just something? An alibi when I didn't even want one."

"And why didn't you want one?" Jack said. "Folks aren't usually eager to do jail time. Most of the people we meet are more inclined to try to run away from a conviction than welcome it."

She shrugged. "I'm not most people."

Jack consulted his notes. "I see you left Chicago after your son died."

"I had nothing to keep me there. No business. No family. No reason to stay. I like the diving here, the fresh air, et cetera."

Jack consulted his notes again. "You catch abalone and sell the meat and shells?"

"Yes. I'm sorry to disappoint, but I do it the right way, keep to my limit and no scuba tanks. Believe it or not, I respect wildlife. I'm not about to deplete the ecosystem for my own profit."

Nate huffed into his mustache. "When did you take up mountain climbing?"

Roxie looked startled. "What?"

The easygoing smile never left Nate's face. "Mountain climbing. You made it to the top of Mt. McKinley in twelve days. That's awesome."

"You are thorough, I'll give you that. After my son died, I realized how quickly it can all go away so I decided to cut loose. I climbed in high school and college so it wasn't too huge a learning curve."

"But with one kidney," Jack said. "Amazing."

A brief smile lit her face. "Yes, it was amazing. It was the last amazing thing that's happened to me in a long while and probably ever will again. Sometimes I look at the pictures just to prove to myself I really did it."

"Do you know a lot about knot tying?"

"Some. Why?"

Jack showed her a picture of the knot.

She shrugged. "Sort of figure eight knot. Not one I would use."

"Why?"

"It's bulky. Why do you ask?"

Jack waited a second. "It's the knot we found around Reggie's neck."

Her mouth fell open. "He was strangled?"

Nate nodded. "Yup."

"So he really was murdered?"

"Really," Nate repeated.

Her face settled back into its expressionless mask. "What do you know? All that trouble finally caught up to him. I guess there is justice for some people."

After a few more routine questions, Jack told Roxie she was free to leave.

She smiled at the detective and officer. "Well, I guess that means there's a murderer here in Finny. To think I moved here for some peace and quiet."

Nate watched her go. "Well, Reggie found his peace

and quiet. Too bad it came at the end of a rope."

Jack suppressed a shudder as he picked up the phone. "Yeah, too bad."

His fingers trembled a little as he dialed.

Bobby, Bobby. She was embedded in his heart and thoughts.

Thinking about her on the other end of the line made his breath catch. She picked up after the third ring.

"Hello?"

"Good morning, Bobby, it's Jack."

"Hi, Jack."

"What's up?"

"I'm headed over for my shift at Uncle Monk's. What's up with you?"

"Working."

"Finding the guy who tried to run Aunt Ruth down, I hope."

"Trying as hard as I can."

She sighed, a soft, fluttery sound. "Good. I think that person needs to do hard time in a rock quarry or something."

"Well, we don't have a rock quarry that I'm aware of, but I'll see what I can do. So, uh, Bobby, I wanted to, to ask you—"

"Yes?"

"If you. . .wanted to show me some diving techniques."

She laughed and then grew quiet. "You're serious."

"Yes."

"Today?"

"Sure. We could grab some lunch after."

"No, Jack."

His heart fell. "Why not?"

"Two reasons. One, diving isn't something you learn on the fly. You need to take a class with a certified instructor. And two, I guess you've been inside all morning, but there's a storm coming in. Looks like a good one. Not diving weather."

He felt slightly relieved. No diving meant she wouldn't have a reason to hang out with Ethan, either. "That makes sense. How about lunch anyway?"

"I need to work that shift so Monk can check on Ruth. Maybe another time."

Her tone made it clear. There would not be another time. He'd blown it. "Look, Bobby—" The words tangled themselves up inside him, refusing to come out.

She finally broke the awkward silence. "I have a question for you."

"Fire away."

"Where is Ethan? You didn't arrest him, did you?"

"No. As a matter of fact I need to talk to him."

"Me, too."

Jack stifled the urge to slam a hand on the desk. "What about?"

"Nothing important. He was supposed to meet me last night, and he never showed up."

15

Ruth wasn't sure if it was the nightmare that awakened her in the predawn hours of Tuesday morning, or the strange flittering movement in her womb. Monk sat bolt upright at her soft moan. He listened and stroked her back as she told about the car bearing down on her and Bryce amidst a squabble of clamoring birds. He fetched a cool cloth for her sweaty brow and brought the glass of orange juice she craved.

She settled back in bed, his big hand laid protectively on her shoulder, and fell into a more restful sleep until the phone rang at seven a.m.

"Hi, Nana Ruth. Is the baby here?" Cootchie's breathing sounded loud across the phone lines.

Ruth sat up, a joy growing inside. She smiled, picturing the wild-haired little girl, and a happy warmth infused her.

"Hello, Cootchie. No, the baby isn't here yet, but guess what?"

"What?"

"It's two babies. I'm going to have twins." For the first time it felt a bit less like a curse and more like a blessing.

The girl let out a cry. "Two babies? How do they fit? Does Uncle Monk have one in his tummy?"

Ruth covered the phone and repeated the comment to Monk, who was up and dressed. He laughed.

"You tell her my stomach is all muscle, no baby."

Ruth chatted with her adopted granddaughter,

feeling again the hole created by her absence. "How are you getting along in Arizona with Grandma Meg?"

"She's made me a sandbox, but there's no worms in the sandbox. Mommy wants to talk. Love you, Nana."

"Love you, too, angel." Ruth swallowed against the tears until Dimple came on the line.

"Hello, Ruth. Greetings of the morning."

"Greetings right back at you, Dimple." The woman had never seemed to give up her pattern of speaking in fortune cookie phrasing. Ruth filled her in on the twin situation.

"Twins? That will mean one for Cootchie to hold and one for me."

"Sort of a buy one, get one free bonus. How are things in Arizona?"

"Dry. I'm just about finished."

"Finished with what?"

"Packing. To come home."

Ruth's breath caught. "To—to come home? To Finny?"

"Yes. I am eager to get back to the mushroom farm."

Dimple was the owner of Pistol Bang's Mushroom Farm, which had lain idle since she left town after Cootchie's brief abduction. Ruth was almost too overwhelmed with emotion to speak. "I didn't think you'd be coming back so soon."

"Cootchie will start school next fall. I should have the mushroom farm back up and running by then. Don't you think?"

Ruth tried not to squeal with glee. "Oh yes. That's very sensible."

"I hear there has been another murder in Finny. Are

you involved this time, too, Ruth? It seems these things have a way of coming home to roost on your doorstep."

Thinking about the near accident two days before, she couldn't stifle the shiver that crept up her spine. "It doesn't involve me too much this time, I'm happy to say. When will you be back?"

"We will stay until after the surfing tournament at the end of the month."

Ruth wracked her brain, thinking about desert surfing. "Um, I didn't think there was much surfing in Arizona."

"It's Cootchie's idea. She's invited all the neighborhood kids to come for a party on Grandma Meg's lawn. She intends to set up a Slip 'N Slide and serve doughnuts and mung bean sprouts." Dimple paused for a moment. "I think perhaps the surfing part is an exercise in visualization."

Ruth laughed. "If anyone can make a bunch of desert dwellers visualize the ocean, it's Cootchie. I can't wait to see you both."

"We are anxious, too, especially to meet the babies. Have you thought of names?"

"Not yet."

"I will put my mind to it and share my thoughts next time we talk."

What would Monk think about a woman who christened her daughter Cootchie having a hand in picking his kids' names? She hung up with a lighter heart. "They're coming home," she told Monk with a rush of joy.

He hugged her. "I'm so glad. It's been far too long since we've seen our Cootchie, and Dimple, too. What can I fix my fine lady for breakfast?"

She glanced at the clock. "Nothing. You're supposed

to be at work, remember? Earning the money to pay for this arsenal of baby supplies?"

"My job today is to take care of you since Bryce is out of town."

Bryce had left for his overnight trip to San Francisco to meet with a lawyer.

What followed was a fierce argument carried out in very civilized tones. It concluded with Ruth's final statement. "Well, if you need to have me in your line of sight all day, then I'm just going to go to the shop with you. At least that way you'll get some work done and maybe I can help in some way."

He sighed. "All right, you can come but no helping, just resting and relaxing."

Figuring that was the best she was going to get, she quickly dressed, rolled up the remaining pages of her script, and slipped them into her coat pocket before they headed off.

Monk conceded to at least let her stop at the Buns Up Bakery for a cinnamon roll, when the morning sickness let up. They ducked into the store and out of the light drizzle. As Al delivered his treasure along with a carton of milk, she noticed Monk casting anxious glances at the people waiting on the wet sidewalk outside his shop door for it to open.

She sat firmly at a table. "Go. I will eat my roll and walk carefully over to your shop after looking both directions twice. I promise."

He folded his arms, brow wrinkled in thought. "Well, I guess it would be okay for you to stay here for a few minutes, but I don't want you crossing by yourself. Call me when you're ready and I'll escort you." Half reluctantly, half eagerly, he went.

Feeling like a five-year-old, Ruth settled into munching with a sigh of relief. The clouds were gathering into a solid gray wall outside. She pulled the stretched and misshapen sweater around her and attacked her carbohydrate missile with vigor.

Dr. Soloski came in and ordered an herbal tea.

"Oh, good morning, Mrs. Budge. Your husband's shop was closed so I came here. Someone told me you had some trouble Sunday night. Are you okay?"

"Yes, I'm fine. Probably just a careless driver. No harm done."

"That's good." He cast a nervous glance out the window.

"Won't you sit down and join me?" Ruth pushed out a chair.

"No, I really should be getting back to work." A tall figure with wiry hair stalked past the window, in the direction of the dentist's office. He shrank a little as Ellen sailed by without noticing him. "On second thought, it wouldn't hurt to take a few minutes." He slid into the chair. "I've been meaning to ask you something anyway."

"Go ahead."

"Ellen says you're working with the college man. Ethan, I think his name is, on a project of some sort."

"Yes, he's filming a documentary."

"I just wondered—not my place to say really—"

"What is it?"

"Well, is he taking underwater footage?"

"He says he isn't. After Reggie, uh, died, he promised

they wouldn't be attempting anything in the ocean."

"Odd. I've seen him in the water twice now, near sunset. Foolish, if you ask me. The waves are rough and visibility is poor with the thick kelp forest we've got here. It's purely suicide to think about a night dive."

"You're not the first person who has noticed him diving. Maybe it's recreational. Are you sure it was Ethan?"

"I guess it could have been someone else. Young, fairly trim male." He shook his head and straightened his glasses. "I shouldn't spend time on worrying about somebody else's problems."

Ruth noticed the shadows under his eyes and the pale cast to his thin face. "Forgive me for saying so, but you look tired. Is everything okay with your sister?"

He heaved a sigh. "As okay as it gets. She's been disabled since birth, a child in a grownup body. I go to see her as often as I can, but she's generally out of it most of the time. She has respiratory issues as well and a load of other complaints that I won't bore you with."

"Oh dear. How awful for you both."

"I've gotten used to it. Jane was seventeen when mother died, so I've been on duty since then."

Ruth couldn't hide her surprise. "Then your sister is quite young."

"She'll be twenty-one next month. Mother didn't think she could have any more children. Jane was her miracle child, disabled or not."

Ruth thought she detected a hint of jealousy in his voice. "It must have been quite a shock."

He sipped some tea. "Mmm. I was in my early twenties when she was born. My parents persuaded me to give up the tree business and start on something more respectable, so I changed directions and went to dental school."

"That's a big switch."

He gave a rueful smile. "I miss it, but it was a practical decision. Hospital bills aren't cheap and insurance will only take you so far." His face brightened. "Things will be better next month, though. Janey's trust fund kicks in when she's twenty-one." He laughed. "Maybe then I'll be able to take up tree climbing again."

He said good-bye and headed out, with a cautious look around first.

Tree climbing might be a big help with Ellen on the loose, Ruth thought as she wiped her sticky fingers and dutifully dialed Monk to escort her across the street.

⚓

The soothing smells of chowder and baking bread surrounded her in the cozy corner of Monk's shop. He had no catering job that day, so the lunchtime crowd would have to suffice. The late morning sky was thick with storm clouds, which she hoped would help spur any passersby to come in for soup. Ruth eased the window open a crack to let in the sharp tang of sea air and let out the rich aromas to attract some customers.

In spite of her husband's baleful looks, she had wiped down the counters, tidied the remaining tray of breakfast scones, and refilled all the jugs of milk and creamer before Monk propelled her into a chair, demanding that she "take a load off."

Though she didn't like to admit it, it did feel good to

settle her girth into a chair and sip tea. Her lively onboard cargo had settled for the moment so she could concentrate on finishing Indigo's journal without distracting kicks to the midsection.

> *Though I never would have conceived of it, I am beginning to think of this windswept corner of the world as my home. Hui and I have labored long and hard with endless cooking and cleaning and our efforts have been rewarded. Though my back aches by day's end and Hui's hands are chapped and hardened, the work is a blessing. This is the only country in the world, I think, where a woman receives anything like just compensation for her work, even though they still believe me to be a man.*
>
> *I learn new things from Hui every day. He has some queer customs from his homeland. Bathing, for one. He insists on cleaning himself in an old tin basin before every meal and changing his clothes. Though he has not much to wear, he will put on the cleanest of his tunics and sit down solemnly before we sup. This is certainly a wonder as most Americans I am told bathe only once or twice a year. I settle for washing my face and hands and a twice weekly dip in an isolated pond we've found in our explorations. Hui climbs a tree and keeps watch when I bathe, sounding a whistle at the approach of any strangers.*
>
> *I bartered with some newcomers to the mining fields who agreed to assist us with our carpentry needs in exchange for two square meals a day and*

any mending they might require. They cut down pine trees and made shakes for a cabin. It's a bit drafty, but oh the bliss of sleeping at night with a roof to keep out the rain and animals. It is grander than any palace indeed. I've begun to put together a rag rug for the floor, and though I have not convinced Hui to sleep in a cot, he has strung a hammock for himself in the corner where he sleeps soundly.

Our typical day goes as follows: Before the sun comes up, Hui starts the water boiling for coffee and tends to the cooking fire. We take a minute to give our thanks to the Lord or "the sky Father" as Hui calls Him, and eat some bread and drink a cup of Hui's tea to break our fast. Then I begin with biscuits, fried potatoes, and pounds of broiled steak and liver. It seems like mountains of food until the miners plunk down their money, sit at our rough board tables, and gulp it down in minutes.

When the men have gone off to their duties, we start on dinner. I prepare six to eight loaves of bread, pies if there are berries to fill them, and whatever kind of meat there is to boil. This week I cooked a pot of chili seasoned with bear meat I bought from a trapper passing through. Abuela would never believe her chili recipe would be feeding a score of rough and tumble miners. Though the pot was enormous, they ate every morsel and even sopped their bread in the vessel to soak up every last drop.

The men seem to like their chili hot, spiced

*with jalapeños and onion the way Abuela would
have prepared it herself. After spending the day
knee deep in icy water, I imagine they welcome
anything that will bring them warmth. Never have
I received so much joy from cooking for people. The
Orsons enjoyed their meals but not with the relish
and zeal of someone half starved. It is true there is
no better seasoning than hunger.*

*If the weather permits and he can find them,
Hui and I enjoy some seasoned abalone. Ah, it is
pure joy to eat the soft strips, bathed in garlic and
butter. There are not many, as they grow so very
slowly, so we keep this small treat for ourselves.
The shells we use to hold our money, strapping two
together and hiding them in the hollow space under
the floor. Hui laughs, telling me our lowly abalone
now hold pearls of great price like their fancy oyster
cousins. I smile to think of it as I read to Hui from
Matthew 13:45–46.*

"Again, the kingdom of heaven is like unto
a merchant man seeking goodly pearls. Who,
when he found one pearl of great price, went
and sold all that he had, and bought it."

*Our strange treasure abalones will soon be
enough to start a little restaurant. I have been
looking at a stove in town, and it will not be long
before I can buy it outright. Then we shall have
a proper kitchen for cooking, and I will know
that Hui's future will be more secure. We are truly
blessed, praise be to God and the Son. My only
sadness comes when I look out on the great wide*

ocean and think of the Orsons. How I wish I
could change the terrible moment when Señor and
Señora Orson were sent to the bottom with no help
from their ▮▮▮▮▮▮▮▮▮▮▮▮ .

Ruth peered more closely at the paper. The words had been blacked out with ink. Were they like that all the time? She couldn't remember. She pulled the paper close until her nose almost touched the paper. What did it say? And more importantly, why would Sandra and Ethan want to conceal it?

16

The sound of clanking tools and muttered complaints woke her from her nap that afternoon. She wrapped up in a sweater against the sudden chill and found Monk, crouched next to a pile of parts that was supposed to somehow morph into a baby swing.

He looked up and gave her an aggravated smile. "We should have paid extra and had this thing put together for us. I'm a cook, not a mechanic."

She patted him, ignoring the swell of nausea in her stomach. "You've got a few more months, honey." The thought sent her into quivers of fear. In a few months she would be the proud parent of two babies. Two. Babies. At her age. The cacophony of fear and doubt started again in her head.

"Lord," she whispered, "help me. Help me to want this."

The phone rang, and she settled onto the sofa to try and relax. Monk's voice grew tense as he talked. Something was wrong. It was written all over his worried face. When he hung up, he came to sit down next to her.

"That was my brother Dave. It's Dad again."

Ruth reached for his hand. "Tell me what happened."

"He was behaving like a stubborn fool and went and climbed a ladder. Fell off and dislocated his shoulder." Monk rubbed a hand over his face. "They've got to get the first apple crop in this weekend, and my brother can't do it all by himself."

She didn't have to think twice. "Go. Go help your father."

Monk ignored her. "Dave tried to hire on some guys

but everyone is hustling their crops in and he can't find any help."

Ruth gently turned his chin to face her. "Go help your brother, Monk. I'll be fine."

He frowned. "No. I can't. Wait a minute. Maybe I can. Why don't you come with me? I'll close up shop and we'll go for a while. It'll be a mini vacation."

Ruth smiled. "Honey, I love you, but I'm not up for a trip to Kansas right now. It's bad enough throwing up every few hours, but doing it on a plane is just too much for me. Besides, I need to make sure Carson finishes that nursery or we're going to have to put the babies in the kitchen sink."

His face clouded over. "Then I'm not going. I can't leave you, not with some nutcase on the loose. You could have been killed by that crazy driver."

"Tell you what. How about I ask Bobby to stay with me until Bryce gets back? I can go to the shop with her in the daytime and help, and she'll be here at night to stay with me."

Monk looked anguished. "Ruth—"

"I know. You love me and I love you, too. I will be safe, and if I feel the least bit nervous, I will go to stay with Mrs. Hodges and Alva can stand in for bodyguard or I can sleep at the police station under Nate's desk. How's that?"

He looked unconvinced as she struggled to her feet. "Where are you going?"

"To make sure you've got enough clean clothes to pack."

True to her word, after Monk booked a last-minute flight

and rushed to the airport, Ruth spent the late afternoon at the shop with Bobby. They chatted while they set things to rights for the next day. The air was heavy with the promise of the approaching storm as they headed home. Ruth filled Bobby in on the cryptic Indigo Orson passages.

Ruth let them into the house, and Bobby set to work making grilled cheese sandwiches for dinner.

"That's an incredible story. I've heard only bits and pieces from Ethan about it."

Ruth shot her a look. "Is he a close friend of yours?"

She laughed. "You sound like Jack. No, not a close friend. We dive together sometimes. Mind if I have a look at that script?"

"Not at all. Sandra is supposed to be picking it up soon, so you'd better look while you have the chance."

Bobby went over the pages while Ruth showered. Clean and wrapped in a warm robe, she found Bobby still peering closely at the inked out words.

"I wish we could make them out." She held the paper close to the lamp.

Seeing Bobby silhouetted in lamplight sparked a thought in Ruth's brain. "I've got an idea." She took the paper and held it to the light, peering at it from the underside. Her pulse quickened. "The copied words are slightly lighter than the ink that was used to cover them up. From this angle I can make out a few of the letters. There's a *W* and later a—what is that?"

Bobby knelt on the floor. "It's two words, I think. The first three letters are *Whi* and the second begins with a *Q*."

They sat back and pondered. Bobby chewed her

fingernail thoughtfully. "The first word has to be *while* or *white* or something like that. What about the second?"

"The Q has to be followed by a U to make sense in English, so what could that be? *Quite? Quack? Queer? Quince?*"

"Queens," Bobby said with a snap of her fingers. "I think it's queens."

Ruth nodded. "White Queens."

They both smiled. "So Señor Orson's precious cargo was a bunch of white queens?" Bobby giggled. "Sounds like something from Alice in Wonderland."

"Yes." Ruth sighed. "Just another mystery to solve."

She was just booting up the computer in the bedroom to do some cyber sleuthing when there was a knock at the door. It was a breathless Alva, wet from the rain. He clutched a hand to his heart. "Evening, ladies. I come to tell ya Paul's been hurt."

Ruth's heart dropped. "What? How? Is it bad?"

"Don't know. Louella said he done fall down the stairs. Jack's on his way back from Half Moon Bay, but his car's given out so Nate went to get 'im." Alva sucked in another deep breath. "Louella told me to go get Bobby."

Bobby was already pulling on a jacket. "Where's Paul?"

"At the hospital."

Bobby looked at Ruth. "Uncle Monk wouldn't want you to be here alone. Come with me."

"Never mind that. I'll stay with her." Alva hitched up his pants. "Don't you worry none. I'm on the case." He marched into the house and immediately checked all the kitchen windows to be sure they were locked before he opened the cupboards mumbling something about candy.

Bobby hugged Ruth. "I'll be back as soon as I can."

"Take care of Paul and call me as soon as you know anything."

She nodded and headed into the rainy night.

Alva made himself at home on the couch. Ruth fixed him some hot cocoa with extra marshmallows and turned on the TV to an old *Howdy Doody* show. Alva sipped happily.

Ruth's stomach was in knots thinking about Paul. She prowled the house for a while, straightening pillows and rinsing a cup left in the sink. "Come on, Ruth," she muttered to herself. "It could be awhile before Bobby can call you."

She returned to the computer and typed in *white queens*. Nothing helpful emerged on the screen. She thumbed through the journal pages to find any tidbit that might help refine her search. Before the computer finished cogitating, there was another knock at the door.

Alva stared into the peephole. "Whatcha want? Do ya know the password?"

"No," Sandra's voice was muffled by the door.

Alva scrunched up his face. "Coming to think of it," he muttered, "I durnt know it either."

"It's okay, Alva. Sandra is here for her journal."

He returned to his show, and Ruth opened the door and invited Sandra in.

"No thanks, Mrs. Budge. I'm here for the binder, then I've got to go."

Ruth handed it over. "I wondered about something. What are the White Queens?"

Sandra dropped the binder and it snapped open, sending papers all over the floor. With much effort, Ruth helped her pick them up. She repeated her question.

Sandra shoveled up the pages in a sloppy pile. "White queens? I don't know. Never heard of them."

"Really? I thought they had something to do with Señor Orson."

Sandra gathered up an armful of untidy papers. "Señor Orson? Um, no, not that I know of. I've really got to go. Thanks so much." She darted down the walkway, leaving Ruth to slowly close the door.

"Jumpy little chicken," Alva called from the couch. "She could use a nap or something."

Ruth retrieved several sheets of the journal that had slipped under the kitchen table. After refilling Alva's cocoa cup and making sure the phone was in reach, she padded back to the computer. There was still nothing on the screen that shed any light on the mystery. She thumbed through the papers in her lap, looking for some unusual tidbit. One passage jumped out at her.

> *The traveler gave them dried tortoise, too. Most had never seen a tortoise, alive or dead, but that did not stop them from eating every speck of it.*
>
> *It reminded me of the strange animals Señor Orson told of when he returned from Australia before our disastrous voyage on the* Triton. *If there were kangaroos in California, they would be hopping for their lives to escape the stew pot.*

She added Australia to her search terms. The answer materialized in front of her eyes in a moment. The title of the article was "AUSTRALIA'S WHITE QUEENS: LOST TREASURE."

*Australia's most precious treasures really are
down under. The rare Pinctada maxima, or South
Sea oyster pearl, must be dived for in a select
number of deep ocean habitats, many of them
off the coast of Australia. The work is extremely
difficult and dangerous yet the rewards are
enticing.*

Ruth sat up straighter and read on.

*The most legendary set of South Sea pearls
was dubbed the White Queens for their enormous
size and glorious sheen, believed to weigh in at
a whopping four hundred seventy carats each.
Owned by merchant Wesley Marble, they were
reportedly purchased by an unknown traveler in
1851 for an exorbitant sum and were never heard
of again. Today's valuation would put the White
Queens' worth at close to five million dollars.*

Ruth knocked over her teacup with a clank.

Alva sat up, his eyes wild. "Whatsa matter? Is it an invasion?"

She fetched some paper towels to mop up the spill. "No, Alva. I was just doing some research. It's okay."

Grumbling, he settled back on the sofa.

The phone rang, startling her again.

"It's me, Aunt Ruth."

She could hear the worry in Bobby's voice. "What is it? How is Paul?"

"They're taking him in for a CAT scan now to check

for head injuries. He has a broken wrist. Jack hasn't made it here yet. I'm sorry, but it looks like I'm going to be staying for a while."

"Of course. Don't you worry about anything here. Alva is keeping me company." She pictured little Paul, scared and in pain, and her eyes filled with tears. Unconsciously, she pressed a hand to her abdomen. "Bobby, I'm going to pray for you all."

"Thank you. I'm praying here, too." There was a tremor in Bobby's voice as she said good night.

Ruth turned to give Alva the news, but he was snoring soundly. She covered him with a warm blanket and headed for the bedroom. Her thoughts were spinning in all directions. Worry about Paul warred with the strange information that had come to light from her research.

Señor Orson's treasure was a set of priceless pearls, the White Queens. She was sure of it just as she was equally sure Ethan and Sandra were trying to recover them. The note she'd found inside the binder proved it. *P. max, 468c and 470c* referred to the species name and carat weight. It could be nothing else.

She snuggled under the down comforter, all the while mulling it over. Reggie must have known what Ethan and Sandra were there for. Had he gotten too close to the treasure and they killed him? Or was there another party interested in the fantastic horde?

Monk called as she settled into bed. She told him about Paul.

"Oh sakes. Is the little guy going to be all right?"

"We'll know soon," Ruth said, hoping Monk wouldn't ask to speak to Bobby. There was no point in worrying

Monk by telling him Alva was currently serving as her bodyguard.

Monk sounded exhausted. "I got in okay. We didn't get much done before sundown, but we'll hit it hard tomorrow morning. We're going to have the crop in by week's end."

"Take care of yourself, honey. I don't want you to hurt anything."

He laughed. "I should be saying that to you. Give yourself a hug for me and pat our little bundles, okay? I love you."

"I love you, too, Monk." She hung up and whispered a prayer for her soul mate in Kansas and the little boy in Finny's only hospital. In spite of her anxiety, the sound of the rain soothed her until her eyelids grew heavy, so heavy that her brain did not register the flash of headlights, quickly extinguished as a car pulled into the shadows outside.

17

Jack was about to explode. He'd gotten a frantic call from Louella about Paul falling down the stairs. He heard from the hospital that Paul's condition was uncertain. And that was it. The uncertainty was killing him. Again he pounded a fist on the roof of his car, water streaming down his windbreaker.

"Piece of junk," he bellowed to the empty, rain-slicked street, straining again to catch a glimpse of Nate's car.

A cab approached from the opposite direction. Jack reached for his badge, ready to commandeer the vehicle, just when Nate screeched up to the curb. Jack jumped in and they took off, as fast as was safe through the storm. He gave Nate a look.

"No word yet, man. They gave Louella a sedative. Bobby's there."

He felt a surge of relief. "Thank You, God," he whispered. At least Paul was not alone. There was someone there he knew and loved. He pulled out his cell and dialed Bobby's number.

She answered on the first ring. "Jack, I've been trying to call you, but the reception is bad here. Paul is having a CAT scan. We'll know more in a little while."

"Bobby—" His throat closed around the words.

"I haven't been able to see him yet. I'll stay right here until I do."

"Okay, thanks." He clicked the phone off.

They didn't speak as they flew back towards Finny.

Nate drove like a man possessed and both were silent for most of the trip. Before the car fully stopped, Jack was out and pounding up the steps into the building. Bobby looked up from her pacing and ran to him until they were wrapped together in a wet, drippy hug. "Thank you for being here," he whispered in her ear.

She swallowed. "It's Paul. Where else would I be?"

He could see the tears in her eyes when he let her go and began to prowl the hallway. "How long could it take to do a CAT scan?"

"The doctor said he'd be done soon."

Nate joined them a few minutes later and handed Jack a dry shirt. "Mary's bringing you a change of clothes when she can, but this will have to do for now."

By the time Jack emerged wearing the shirt, Nate had three cups of steaming coffee for them. Though he didn't feel like drinking it, he did anyway, letting the liquid burn the reality into him.

Paul was hurt. The wrist was the least of their problems. Jack had seen enough accidents in his career to know what a head injury could mean. Paralysis. Brain damage. Death. What would he do if Paul died, too?

The thought made him shudder.

He got up again to pace the floor, willing the doctor to come out and tell him, tell him what they hadn't been able to when they'd brought Lacey in. Bobby and Nate sat in silence, watching him. They came to stand beside him when a surgeon in green scrubs approached.

Jack's mouth went dry. He tried to speak but nothing came out.

After what seemed like an interminable pause, the

doctor spoke. "Paul has sustained a concussion, but not a major one. The wrist will have to be seen by an orthopedist, but it doesn't look like a complicated break. We'll keep him overnight, but I think he'll be just fine."

Jack gripped him by the hand so hard the surgeon winced. "Thank you. Thank you very much."

Bobby sighed loudly. "Is Louella going to be all right?"

The physician smiled. "Absolutely, but she can stay the night, too. She'll be fine once the sedative wears off. I don't think she's going to let Paul use the stairs anytime soon."

Jack felt light-headed with relief. "When can I see him?"

"Give the nurse a few minutes and then you can go in." He waved as he left them.

Jack flopped into a chair. Nate gripped his arm. "I've gotta go back to the shop. Mary's by herself." He gave a last squeeze and exhaled, the breath ruffling his mustache. "Good deal, man. Good deal."

Jack nodded, hearing the unspoken emotion in his partner's voice. "Thanks, Nate."

"You bet."

Jack checked on Louella, who was sleeping, fortunately. There would be an emotional storm when she woke up, he knew. He returned to the waiting chairs and sat down next to Bobby. The hallway settled into silence.

Bobby checked her watch. "It's so late. I hate to disturb Aunt Ruth, but I know she's waiting for my call." She dialed the number. "Busy signal. She must be talking to Uncle Monk. I think I'll wait to see Paul, if that's okay with you, and then I'll take off."

He reached out a hand to hers. "Of course it's okay. I wanted to say, to tell you, how much it means to Paul that you were here for him." *And to me. Say it, you idiot. Tell her what she means to you.* The emotion choked off his words.

Bobby nodded. "I know. You don't have to thank me."

He sighed. "I hate the smell of this place. It's like it's burned into my brain. Every time I come here I get a whiff of the cleaner or whatever it is they used the day my wife died. They probably don't even use that kind anymore, but it still smells the same to me."

"But this time you got good news. Your son is going to be fine."

He leaned against the wall and closed his eyes. He'd never been so completely exhausted in his entire life. "I don't know what I would have done if the news had been different. Losing Paul would be—" He couldn't finish.

Bobby took his hand and prayed out loud. "Father, thank You for watching over Paul. Thank You for keeping him in Your loving hands and delivering him safely from this accident. Bring Your peace down on all of us, Lord, and receive our deepest gratitude."

Jack spoke the amen along with her.

Soon the nurse ushered them in to see the boy. He looked pale and small in the big hospital bed, a purple bruise showing on his forehead. Jack stroked his hair. "Hi, buddy. I heard you took a fall. Does your wrist hurt?"

Paul shook his head, eyes half closed. "Uh-uh."

"That's good. I was worried there for a little bit." Jack blinked back the moisture in his eyes. "Miss Louella is sleeping here tonight in the room next door. Bobby is here to see you, too."

Bobby kissed Paul lightly on the cheek. "Hey, kiddo. You're supposed to wear a helmet if you're going to fall down the stairs."

Paul smiled and slipped into sleep. Jack and Bobby took up positions in the chairs. Jack tried to think of a line of conversation that would keep her there, near him, near them both.

"You were right about the wreck, by the way."

She blinked. "What?"

"That's why I went to Half Moon Bay. I talked to a salvage guy there who is also a history buff and he agrees with you. The *Triton* was a big bucket of coal, no treasure that would pique the interest of any profit seekers. I guess I owe you an apology."

"You might owe Ethan one, but I'm not so sure anymore."

It was his turn to blink. "Why?"

"Aunt Ruth's journal, the one Ethan and Sandy gave her. It refers to some sort of treasure called the White Queens, though the words were blacked out."

"What's a White Queen?"

"I don't know, but Aunt Ruth was on the case when I left to come here."

He laughed. "Leave it to my two favorite women to ferret out another mystery. Do you think that's what Ethan and Sandy are diving for?"

"I don't know. I would rather not think of Ethan as a liar, but it does seem suspicious."

He took a deep breath. "If it does turn out to be true, I'm sorry. I know Ethan is a friend of yours and I probably haven't given him a fair chance."

She shrugged. "I'm sure he's got reasons for what he's been up to. I'm going to step out into the hall and try Aunt Ruth again."

Jack watched the steady rise and fall of Paul's chest, more

beautiful to him than the mesmerizing ebb and flow of the ocean waves. He was overwhelmed with an enormous sense of gratitude. God spared his son. He did not yet understand why the Lord took Lacey, and he probably never would. But Jack had Paul, and he would die to keep the boy safe and happy.

Bobby returned with a frown on her face. "Still busy. I think I'd better go home and check on things." She walked to Paul's bed and stroked a finger lightly down his cheek. "I am so glad you're safe, kiddo," she whispered.

The sight of them there, heads bent close together, filled up his soul. Jack's own voice came out in a whisper. "You really love him, don't you?"

She continued to gaze at the boy's face for a moment before she turned her attention to Jack. Sadness washed over her fine features. "I do love him, a little bit more every day." She looked Jack squarely in the eyes. "That's why I'm taking the job in Utah."

~

The lancing pain in Jack's chest did not go away, even after Bobby had headed off to Ruth's. She was leaving, for good. He should have run after her, but he didn't. He stayed, rooted to the dingy tile floor, watching her vanish through the doorway.

He felt a flare of anger. How could she leave? She loved Paul and he loved her. Was it fair to pick up and take off? The anger was quickly overtaken by despair. Why should she stay? Just to be a friend to somebody else's kid? She had given him everything: friendship, sympathy, support, and he had given her nothing in return.

He scrubbed a hand through his cropped hair. He'd thought the problem was the guilt he felt about committing to another woman after Lacey, but the revelation came to him in a flash. It wasn't guilt. He was afraid, gut-wrenchingly, spine-chillingly afraid to love someone else and lose her as he had his wife.

Paul stirred and mumbled in his sleep. Jack spread the covers more securely over him.

Jack continued to puzzle it over. To love meant, perhaps, to lose. It was a frightening burden to care about someone else so much. But not to love? If he had the choice, would he rather not have a son? This precious kid who kept him awake with worry and wrenched his gut with indecision?

Paul was the greatest thing in his life. To not risk, would mean to not have experienced that overwhelming connection. His head spun. What was he doing? His life was running by in a frenetic blur and the only moments worth savoring were the ones he spent with Paul. And with Bobby.

But could he risk that kind of pain again? For them both? He watched Paul's delicate profile. Could the child withstand losing another woman in his life?

Ruth's face flashed across his mind. She had buried her beloved husband and somehow, somewhere, she'd found the courage to start another life.

He knew he had to talk to her. He needed to find out if he had what it took to love again.

18

Ruth's eyes flew open. She lay there, disoriented. The sound of a fierce storm battered the cottage walls. The time on the bedroom clock read 2:15 a.m. She wondered why Bobby hadn't called. She lifted the receiver to dial the woman's cell.

No dial tone.

"The storm must be messing with the reception," she babbled to herself.

She heard a thunk from the bedroom next door.

Her stomach clenched. Maybe it was Alva looking for something. Or perhaps Bobby had returned. But why would she be in the nursery?

Ruth grabbed a robe and tiptoed out into the hallway, inching her way across the creaky wood floor. She listened. All was quiet. Feeling chilled to the bone, she padded into the living room. There was Alva, snoring on the couch. The door to Bryce's room where Bobby was bunked was open and dark. Again she heard a noise from the nursery.

She searched for her cell phone to call the police. Where was the silly thing? With a sense of rising panic, she went to the sofa and gently shook Alva awake.

"Whaaa?" he said, one eye open. "What's a-goin' on? Is it morning yet? I ain't done sleeping."

"No," Ruth whispered in his ear. "I think someone is breaking in, through the nursery window. The phone is dead, too."

Both of Alva's eyes shot open. "Whazzat? A burglar?

I'll handle this." He leapt off the sofa and charged into the kitchen in search of a weapon. He grabbed the first thing he saw, a crusty baguette, before he began to tiptoe down the hallway.

Ruth tried to restrain him. "Alva, let's get out and call the police."

"You just stay put, sweet cheeks. I'm ex military. I tangled with communists. I can handle it. Whoever it is ain't got nothin' on a commie." He hitched up his baggy trousers and continued stalking toward the bedroom, his socks slipping slightly on the wood.

"This is crazy, Alva. We need to get the police," she hissed. "Come with me."

Alva ignored her. After a moment of deep breathing, he launched himself, shoulder first, at the nursery door.

"No!" Ruth's cry filled the hallway, but it was too late.

The impact of the collision sent Alva's spindly body rebounding back across the space. His head made a hollow *thwop* noise as he came to a stop against the far wall.

She ran to him. "Are you okay?"

He shook his head and pushed her away before he approached the door again, this time trying the knob. It turned easily in his hand.

Ruth's skin prickled all over with goose bumps and she struggled to breathe.

The old man pushed the door open a few inches and stopped, readying the baguette like Don Quixote's spear.

"Don't do it. Please." Ruth's voice rose on a tide of fear. "Alva, no!"

With a deafening howl, he careened through the doorway.

Ruth screamed.

There was a crash and a high-pitched yell.

She ran into the room and flipped on the light.

Bobby lay on her back, covered in bread fragments. Alva sat on his bottom across from her, blinking against the sudden light.

"It's you," they both said at once.

Ruth was too stunned to speak.

"Whatcha doin' in here, Miss Walker?" Alva picked up the ruined baguette and absentmindedly stuck a wad of it into his mouth. "How's Paul?"

Bobby picked herself up in a shower of breadcrumbs. "Paul's got a concussion, but he's going to be okay. Why did you poke me with a loaf of bread?"

"We thought you was a burglar. Heard someone breaking in. Why did ya come in through the window anyways? I wouldn't have mashed you if you used the door."

Ruth was relieved to hear about Paul. She sank down on top of a cardboard box theoretically filled with all the parts necessary to build a playpen. Her knees shook. "It's my fault, Bobby. I heard someone climbing in. I must have imagined it."

"No, you were right. There was someone trying to get in."

Ruth's mouth went dry. "There was?"

Bobby nodded. "I heard someone shout 'no!' from the house, and I figured the fastest way to get in was through the window. Before I could get there, someone jumped out and ran down the street. I saw a car pull out. Sorry if I scared you. Are you two all right?"

Ruth nodded. "I think so, but the thought of someone

breaking in terrifies me. What could they want?"

Bobby shook her head as she helped Alva to his feet. "Something to do with your research maybe?"

A light dawned in Ruth's mind. "Could be. Maybe Sandra noticed the missing pages from her notebook and came back to retrieve them."

Alva snorted. "Woulda been a mite bit easier to ring the doorbell."

Ruth had to agree with him on that point.

She filled Bobby in on her White Queens discovery while they called the police department and waited for Nate to arrive. Ruth contemplated calling Monk, but she decided it would only make him crazy with worry. There was nothing to be done. She was safe, temporarily, with Bobby and Alva for company.

Nate came and left, after dusting for prints and promising to drive by several more times before his shift was over. Mary would take over in the morning. Ruth knew she should get to sleep, but her nerves were on edge. The babies must have been stimulated by her emotions because they kept up a rigorous rolling and tumbling match.

Bobby fixed them both some tea, and Alva fell to snoring on the sofa again.

Ruth watched her from over the rim of her mug, noting the fine crease between her brows. "Bobby, what's wrong? You look like something is bothering you, aside from all this, I mean. Is it Paul's accident?"

She shook the black hair out of her eyes. "Oh, it's nothing. I've—I've decided to take the job in Utah. I told Jack tonight."

Ruth tried to keep her expression neutral. "What did he say?"

"Nothing." The disappointment was evident on her face. "I knew he wouldn't, but still. . ."

"You wished he would have stopped you?"

She sighed. "Yes, but he didn't, and that tells me I'm making the right decision to go. I'm going to stay long enough to wrap things up here. I'll still come and visit as much as I can."

"Things will not be the same here without you. Your uncle will be sad to have you move out of state, and so will I."

Bobby nodded, toying with her mug. The grief and determination revealed themselves on her face.

Ruth measured her words carefully. "I will miss you so very much, but if that's what you think is best, Monk and I will support you."

"Thank you. I've got to make a new beginning. It's time for me to restart my career." She yawned. "I'm going to lie down for a while. It's been a long night. How about you?"

"Yes, I'll try to get some sleep, too." She wondered if Jack Denny would be getting any rest that night.

Bryce and Maude arrived at roughly the same time the next morning, only moments after Bobby left. Maude held a plate of wrapped cookies in her hands. Bryce stepped through the door and kissed his mother, said hello to Maude, and then disappeared.

Ruth did not comment on the angry cast to his face.

Don't pester, she reminded herself. *Don't smother. He'll tell you when he's ready.* She pulled her robe more securely around her middle and offered Maude some coffee.

"No, thank you, Ruth. I'm not ingesting caffeine anymore and you shouldn't, either."

"It's decaf," Ruth said, too tired to defend herself properly. "Please sit down."

"Ahh. Well, I happened to be at the police department this morning and I heard about your burglar. What is the world coming to these days?" She drummed stubby fingers on the table top. "I brought you some cookies."

"Oh, thank you. How considerate. What kind?"

"No fat, high fiber, soy bran cookies."

Ruth tried to look enthusiastic as she put them on the kitchen counter. "Er, thank you. I'll have some later."

Maude looked around and picked at a scratch on the wood. "Ruth, um, I need to ask your advice."

She swallowed her surprise. In all the years she'd known Maude, the woman was vastly more experienced at giving advice than asking for it. "Sure. Go ahead."

"I was wondering, if, you know, I should dye my hair."

Ruth eyed Maude's black bun. "Whatever for?"

"Well, I've got a few grays, you see, and anyway, somebody told me blond is more flattering on an experienced face."

Experienced face? Ruth tried to hide her smile. "Maude, is there by any chance a certain dentist you are trying to impress?"

"Me? Trying to impress Dr. Soloski? Of course not." A pink stain crept into her face. "He's not the kind you could impress easily, anyway. He's old money."

"I thought he was a dentist."

"Funny, Ruth," Maude said with a face that indicated she didn't think it was at all amusing. "Dr. Soloski is from *the* Soloskis. His parents made a bundle in the oil business."

"If he's from wealthy stock, why did he settle here?"

She raised an eyebrow. "To be near his sister, of course. She's an invalid."

"Yes, he told me. He said it's expensive to care for her."

Maude snorted. "He's just being modest. I admire that in a person, don't you? Taking care not to make anyone feel inferior?"

"Oh yes." Ruth looked up to find Alva chomping a cookie he'd taken from Maude's platter.

"Bleccch," he said, spitting it into the sink. "Whaddya call these? Shoe leather cookies? You could use 'em for coasters."

Ruth intervened before Maude could get her hackles up. "Alva, thanks for staying with me. You were a big help last night."

He nodded. "No trouble at all, ma'am. Just doing my job. I'm gonna go home now. Mrs. Hodges will expect me for breakfast."

Alva and Maude exchanged a glare before he left.

"Well, anyway, Maude, I think your hair is fine. It suits you."

"I've always thought so, but everyone needs a change now and then, don't you think?"

"I suppose."

"Maybe auburn instead of blond."

Ruth tried to make her expression encouraging.

"Maybe. So have you been spending much time with Dr. Soloski these days?"

"Oh, not really. We chat a little when we can. I heard from Gene, I mean Dr. Soloski, that Roxie has some sort of health problem. Kidneys or something?"

"Yes. I heard that, too."

Maude lowered her voice. "She's not exactly lily white, you know. I heard her son was a thief and stole from her clients. She tried to take the fall for him and it ruined her. Sad, isn't it? Raising a no-goodnik?"

Ruth thought back to her earlier conversations with Roxie. "Her son died, Maude. I don't think anything he did while he was living would make that loss any easier."

She sniffed. "Maybe, but the whole thing certainly left her penniless. She's a renter, you know."

Maude said the word as if it was a profanity.

Bryce came hesitantly into the kitchen. "Just looking for some breakfast."

Ruth resisted the urge to jump up and make it for him. If she was ever going to get this mothering thing straight for the twins, she'd have to be strong with Bryce. *Don't smother.*

Maude excused herself with a parting shot. "Make sure you keep moisturizing your belly. The stretch marks will be insane with two in there."

Ruth sighed and saw Maude to the door.

Bryce did not seem inclined toward conversation as he fixed himself toast and two fried eggs. The smell drove her from the kitchen along with a sudden recollection that it was the first Wednesday of the month and she needed to take Royland his worm delivery. Burglars or no burglars, she had a business to run. She pulled on some clothes and waddled out into the backyard.

The birds were happy to be released from their fenced area and promptly swarmed around her as she scattered bread cubes and protein pellets onto the ground. That would keep them busy and away from the worms. She added a few of Maude's cookies for good measure, noticing that the birds scrupulously avoided the bits.

The mash she applied to the top of the worm beds sent them into wiggly ecstasy. When they crept to the surface to feed, she scooped up a generous quantity of the squirming soil and put it in the spinner. A few cranks and the drum whirled off most of the dirt, leaving a pile of disgruntled worms at the bottom. She packed them into a breathable plastic bag and covered them with a thin layer of soil to keep them happy on the journey.

Bryce was watching her with a cup of coffee in one hand and a corner of toast in the other. Milton stared at him, dancing up and down on impatient bird feet. Bryce ignored him and finished the toast. "Making a delivery?"

"Yes, it's Royland's day."

"I'll go with you."

"You don't have to."

"Yes, I do. Monk wouldn't want you to go by yourself, and he's not a man I'd want to make unhappy."

She laughed. "Me neither. You should have seen what happened when our summer help decided Monk's chowder needed more pepper."

Bryce smiled. "I'll bet he's not your summer help anymore."

"Exactly." Ruth walked slowly through the gaggle of

birds to the gate, and they began their walk.

The sun shone through pockets of clouds, the ground saturated by the storm the night before. Sunshine warmed her back as they strolled along. She wanted to ask how his trip to San Francisco had gone, but she wasn't sure he'd welcome the inquiry. Instead she filled him in on the burglary attempt.

"Wow, Mom. You sure are attracting someone's attention and not in a good way. What did Monk say about the latest problem?"

She flushed. "He doesn't know yet."

"Oh, I see. If he did, he'd be on the next flight out."

"Or rent a car and get all kinds of tickets driving home at breakneck speed."

"Nice to have somebody love you that much." Bryce kicked at a stone on the sidewalk as they headed out of town.

They both shot an occasional look over their shoulders for oncoming cars. A welcome coolness in the air made the temperature just right for walking. The long winding drive to Royland's farm was damp when they arrived, so they had to pick their way carefully to avoid the sticky spots.

The silence lengthened until she couldn't stand it anymore. "How was your trip to San Francisco?"

"Okay, I guess. I signed the papers Roslyn is so anxious to get. The house can be sold any time. She probably has it up on the market by now." He jammed his hands into his pockets. "I also spoke to an employment agency but that led nowhere. It's so blasted unfair. I ran a company, I don't need to work for somebody and take orders like a high school kid. I've got a degree."

She looked at the petulant jut of his chin. *Oh Bryce. You've got so much to learn.*

He looked at her. "You think I'm being arrogant, don't you?"

Stay quiet, Ruth. Keep your opinions to yourself. "Yes, I do."

His mouth tightened. "I've got skills. I'm a smart guy. Why should I have to start out doing a bunch of grunt work? One trucking outfit wanted me to tidy the office in between assignments."

Now that she'd gone ahead and opened her big mouth, might as well finish it off. "These people don't know you, and they won't until you can prove yourself. Your father started out sweeping and cleaning clinic floors until he got his own office. Nothing is owed to you, Bryce, just because you're intelligent and college educated." She waited for the inevitable fallout of her criticism. Why couldn't she have kept her mouth firmly closed?

Bryce's look gradually changed. A smile crept onto his face. "I thought you were going to say I was so smart I should hold out for something better."

"I wanted to, but I thought the other advice was more helpful."

He laughed. "Sometimes bitter medicine works best, as Dad would have said."

She joined in the laughter until it struck her. "Bryce, are you looking for a job. . .around here? In California?" It couldn't be true after so many years of distance.

Bryce looked up at the ramshackle farm as they approached. "I've got no reason to stay in Chicago. I thought I might stick around for a while, get to know my new brother and sister, or brothers, or sisters."

"That sounds like a great idea to me." Ruth's heart felt lighter than it had in a very long time as they walked together in the sun.

19

Monk was more than perturbed. He about jumped through the phone line when Ruth told him late that afternoon about the break-in.

"What is going on there?" he roared. "You've got to go immediately to the police station and stay there until I get back. I'll book the earliest flight I can find."

She waited for his tirade to wind down. "Honey, I'm not going to go sit in the police station. Bryce is here and Jack is coming over later to talk to me about something. I'm perfectly fine, safe as can be."

"What about the babies? Are they okay? Did the shock of the break-in stunt their growth or anything?"

"Not that I can tell from the kicks to my kidneys. Did you get the crop in?"

"Most of it. Dave can finish it up. Look, Ruthy, I'm going to hang up now and call the airport. Don't go anywhere by yourself, not even out to get the newspaper from the driveway. Those college people are trying to do you in, I just know it. The whole thing makes my skin crawl."

"I'm going to tell Jack all about the White Queens and leave the whole thing up to him. How's that?"

"You promise to stay out of the investigation?"

"I will do my best to keep my nosy tendencies in check."

Monk grumbled. "Well, I guess that will have to do for now, but I'll feel much better when I'm back home."

Ruth hung up thinking the very same thing.

A scant half hour later, Jack arrived. Instead of staying for a visit, he took Ruth on a ride back toward town. "Nate's meeting me at the Finny Hotel. We're going to take Ethan and Sandra in for questioning. I wanted you to stick around and add your two cents on this White Queens thing Bobby told me you figured out. How does that sound?"

"Great, I'd be happy to help. Monk will be relieved that I've got a temporary police escort. He thinks I should be living at the station until he returns."

He laughed. "I wouldn't recommend it. The coffee is terrible. Can I buy you some dinner after?" He tapped his fingers on the steering wheel. "There's, er, something I want to talk to you about."

"Of course." Ruth took a moment to call Bryce and tell him about her plans.

"Okay," he said. "I'll fill Monk in when he calls every half hour. I'm going to go for a run on the beach, but I'll take the cell phone with me."

They pulled up to the Finny Hotel and she waited in the car while Jack and Nate headed inside. Jack returned a few minutes later, a frown on his face. "They checked out this morning."

Nate blew into his mustache. "Yeah, but the clerk said they were carrying dive gear, almost as if they were going to take one last dip before they skipped town."

Jack arched an eyebrow. "Surely they wouldn't do that. I called and told them to wait for me this morning. They know something is up. Why go diving?"

Nate considered. "Maybe they're desperate to find something. Desperate people do desperately stupid things, as we are daily reminded."

"Maybe," Jack said as he got into the car. "How about a quick trip to the beach, Ruth?"

—

Sandra and Ethan were just headed into the choppy water when Jack and Nate pulled up. They stood there, frozen for a moment, the waves lapping around their shins, before exchanging a hurried conversation as the officers approached. Ruth stayed a safe distance behind, but not so far that she couldn't hear every word.

Jack's tone was like iron. "I told you to wait at the hotel."

"Oh, uh, is that what you said? We weren't sure." Sandra's face was milk white where it was framed by the black of her wet suit. They shuffled up to dry ground to meet the officers.

Jack did not return Sandra's smile. "You need to come to the station now."

"Right now?" Ethan said.

"Right now," Jack assured them.

The young man straightened. "Why? What exactly is the reason for this? Are we being arrested?"

"Not yet." Jack smiled at them.

It didn't look like a friendly grin to Ruth.

"Just wanted to chat about a couple of Queens. You have time for that, don't you?"

Sandra and Ethan looked at each other again before they followed Nate to his car, Ruth and Jack a few steps behind.

They must have been granted time to change their clothes after they arrived at the station, Ruth noted, because Sandra joined them in the conference room wearing sweatpants and a long-sleeved shirt. She sat rigid in the chair, fingers laced, knees pressed together. Her throat worked convulsively as she darted a glance around the room. "Where's Ethan?"

Jack offered a cup of coffee, which the woman declined. "He's waiting with Mary. We thought it would be nice to chat with you both separately."

"Um, I'd rather not."

Though his tone was light, Jack's words left no room for compromise. "I think you don't have much choice. I can arrest you, if you'd like, and we can take it from there."

Her eyes rounded in terror. "No, no. I didn't do anything. I didn't commit any crime."

"I asked you before why you were here in Finny and you only told me half the truth. Now tell me the real reason." Jack stared at her from behind his desk. "All of it."

She didn't answer.

Nate gave her a smile. "You'd be better off going along with him, ma'am, otherwise he's going to be stuck to you like duct tape until you come clean. I've seen it before and it's not pretty."

Ruth held her breath to see if the woman would talk.

Sandra cleared her throat. "We didn't do anything wrong. Well, we maybe didn't exactly tell the whole truth, but that's it. We were following the clues from the journal."

"Are you sure Indigo's writing is factual?" Ruth said.

"All the details check out. The life of Indigo Orson is traceable, and believe me, we know because we spent months doing just that."

For some reason which she could not understand, Ruth was relieved that Indigo really did exist.

"Why are you here in Finny?" Jack repeated.

"We really did come to do a reenactment of Indigo's life, but we sort of had another goal in mind, too."

"The White Queens?" Ruth said.

She nodded. "I guess we didn't cover our tracks very well."

"So there really is a set of priceless pearls right under Finny's nose?"

"We believe so. I told you I stumbled on Indigo's journal in an old box in the university basement when we were researching for our project. We did some more checking and all the facts came together. Orson was carrying the pearls when he boarded the *Triton*, as far as we can ascertain."

Jack snorted. "But that was more than 150 years ago."

"As far as history records, the boat was supposedly only carrying coal so it hasn't had a whole lot of attention. Plus it settled at an awkward angle so the lower cabins, where the Orsons stayed, were pretty much inaccessible."

Jack stared at her, with his elbows on the table. "So you decided to recover the pearls yourselves?"

"It was a long shot, but Ethan is a great diver. He talked the Skylar Foundation into giving us some money up front, providing they got their cut of the treasure. They sent Reggie to help, but I really think it was more to keep an eye on us."

As little as she'd seen of Reggie, Ruth was not surprised to hear he was more than just a cameraman.

Jack nodded. "People dove that wreck before. How do you know they didn't recover the pearls and keep it on the lowdown?"

"They didn't know what to look for, for one thing, and the big storm you had last year caused the wreck to shift. According to Ethan's preliminary dive, the movement opened up the under decking for exploration." She toyed with a thread on her pants. "He was sure we would find the pearls."

"What made him so certain?"

Her face crumpled. "Desperation, I think, same as me. The university didn't renew his scholarship for next term, and his family couldn't help him with the tuition. He figured we'd give the research project a good effort and hopefully find the pearls, too. I never could snag a scholarship in the first place, so the idea of finding something that would fund my education seemed like a reasonable gamble."

Nate tapped a pencil on his knee. "Correct me here, but wouldn't the pearls belong to the state government since that wreck is within a three-mile distance of the coast?"

Sandra clamped her lips shut, her face coloring. "It doesn't matter anyway, does it? We didn't find the pearls."

"Did Reggie?"

She started. "Reggie?"

Jack cocked his head. "It would fit. Maybe he found the pearls and decided to take them for himself. One of you strangled him and dumped his body in the ocean."

A shiver rippled Sandra's shoulders. "That was horrible. We didn't kill him. As a matter of fact, we cautioned him against night diving, but Reggie was a, uh, determined person. Ethan tried to keep an eye on him, figuring he'd be happy to double-cross us. The night Reggie went out, Ethan kept watch for hours until he gave up. And anyway, why would we stick around if Reggie had already gotten the pearls and we'd killed him for them?"

Jack leveled a look at her. "Good question, Ms. Marconi. I'd love to hear your answer."

Sandra didn't seem to have an answer. She stuttered to a stop several times before bursting into tears. Nate went to fetch a glass of water. She was dismissed to the waiting room and told to stay in Finny for the next few days.

Ethan's interview was similar in content though much less emotional. "We haven't committed a crime. We should be allowed to go. You have no right to keep us here."

Jack drummed his fingers on the desk. "Did you try to run down Mrs. Budge?"

Ethan blinked but remained expressionless. "No. Why would I do that?"

"Because she figured out the secret of the treasure you're looking for."

He shot her a quick look. "I didn't know that possibility existed until Sandra told me there were missing pages. Frankly, no offense, Mrs. Budge, but I thought the journal was so generic that you wouldn't be smart enough to glean any info about the pearls from it."

Ruth sighed. Round, waxy, and dumb. She really had to work on how she presented herself.

"Did you try to break into her house to retrieve the papers?" Jack continued.

"No." He sighed. "We're probably idiots for thinking we could find those pearls, but we're not criminals, believe it or not."

Ruth believed him, but then again, she reminded herself, she believed everyone.

After another string of questions, Jack dismissed him with the same admonishment he'd given Sandra, along with one other piece of advice. "Stay out of the water."

Ethan gave him a cool look. "I will, but if someone murdered Reggie for those pearls, then we're not the only ones you need to be worrying about."

Jack slouched in the chair after Ethan left. Ruth noticed the tired shadows under his eyes. Paul's accident had taken a toll on him and she was sure Bobby's announcement had, too.

"Thanks for helping out, Ruth. Are you ready for dinner?"

—

He took her to a small café at the edge of town, one busy with locals and visitors. She wondered if he was looking for some background noise to discourage busy ears from listening in. They settled down over bowls of chicken chowder and chopped salads.

"Thanks for having dinner with me. Too bad it's not as good as Monk's soup."

She laughed. "Nothing's as good as Monk's soup."

"True. Monk is an amazing guy, and he's devoted to you."

"Yes. I am very blessed."

Jack looked around the room for the umpteenth time before he finally spoke. "In a way, that's kind of what I wanted to ask you about. You've heard that Bobby is leaving?"

"Yes."

He shifted, toying with the spoon in his hand. "I'll be honest here. I want her to stay, but I'm having trouble giving her a reason. I'm not sure if I can't let go of Lacey or if I'm just a coward about committing to Bobby." He sighed. "I'm a dismal failure in my personal life."

Her heart ached at his painful admission. He looked so confused, a vulnerability creeping over his face that she hadn't seen before. "No, you're not, Jack. If you were, Bobby wouldn't love you."

"I guess. Do you mind if I ask you something personal?"

"Fire away, Detective."

"I just wondered, you know, after Phillip died, how you found closure and everything. How did you put that behind you so you could start a new life with Monk?"

"That's the thing, Jack. I don't think it is a new life. It's just another phase of the one God gave me in the first place. But I admit that I spent years being mad, and devastated, and then a few more feeling guilty for not feeling that way."

He nodded slowly. "I've been trying real hard to figure it out. I loved my wife more than anything, but I know that she wouldn't want me and Paul to be alone. I think it's something else." His forehead creased. "I'm pretty sure that I feel more afraid than guilty."

She covered his hand with hers. "I know that kind of fear, Jack. I've been there, too, and now, at my advanced age, I'm going to bring two more lives into this world with all the worry and fear that entails. If that isn't enough to strike terror into the heart, I don't know what is."

He leaned forward. "So how do you do it? How do you accept that?"

She thought carefully before she answered. "I try to remember Jeremiah 29:11."

He squinted in recollection. " 'For I know the plans I have for you,' declares the Lord, 'plans to prosper you and not to harm you, plans to give you hope and a future.' "

She sat back. "Exactly, and I can tell what you're thinking. We've both already experienced a hefty dose of harm, haven't we? Your wife, my husband."

"That's right."

She took a breath, trying to put into words the sum of a lifetime of love and loss. "But we're still here, Jack. We still have joy and terror and fear, and more joy and bunches more fear. We still have the chance to laugh and hug and weep. We have the great privilege to get up every day and love someone, to show the tenderness to another that God has shown us. As long as we have that chance, we have to take it."

He didn't look convinced. "That's a hard thing to do."

She nodded. "Yes, but if we turned our back on the chance to love, then our lives would be a much greater calamity, a waste of our God-given purpose. There's a reason you are here, beyond your job and your duties. You are here to love other people, and that's just not a safe thing to do, is it?"

He looked at her for a long moment, as if he was solving a puzzle in his mind. Then he grinned, a wide, slow smile that spread over his face in degrees. "Nope, it's a crazy, risky, nutzo thing to do." He laughed. "How did you get so smart, Mrs. Budge?"

"Oh, believe me, Jack. Most of my days are spent in terror about the impending birth of two—count them—two babies. But now and again, God pokes me with a bit of joy and I know He's got my future in His hands and theirs, too." She thought of Bryce and his decision to stay close by, and Cootchie and Dimple's imminent return. An infant elbow, or perhaps a foot, made a tickle in her belly. "Watching Monk try to put together a baby crib provides enough laughter to fill me up for a long while."

Their chuckles were cut short by the chirp of his cell phone.

"Duty calls," he said as he answered it.

She watched his face change. The pleasure gave way to a professional mask, his voice morphed into clipped tones. "I'm on my way."

He clicked off the phone and looked at her. "I'm sorry, Ruth. It's Bryce."

20

Jack drove her to the hospital and supplied her with sketchy facts along the way. Bryce had been found on the beach with a serious head injury.

Ruth felt as though her head was spinning like a carousel. "Did he fall off the cliff?"

Jack gave her a sympathetic look. "I don't know the details, but we'll find out soon."

She sat in numb terror as they completed the drive.

The nurse met them in the waiting area. "There's a lot of swelling in his brain. The doctors are taking some images now to assess the situation."

Assess the situation. Did medical professionals have a book somewhere that taught them how to give information without really telling a person anything? She felt light-headed, and Jack led her to a chair. For the first time Ruth noticed Roxie in the corner, knit cap twisted in her hands.

Her eyes were bloodshot. "Ruth, I'm so sorry. I found your son on the rocks and called the ambulance. Is he going to be okay?"

"The rocks?" Jack came over. "How was he lying? Did you see anyone else around?"

She shook her head. "I was out checking the boat because I just had the motor adjusted and I wanted to see if I got my money's worth. Bryce was lying on his stomach on the bottom of the cliff, the one that the pelicans like to roost on. There was no one with him, but the tide was coming in fast, so I thought I'd better get him out of the water."

Jack's eyes narrowed. "So he was just on his stomach there? Alone? No one else was around?"

"No. Maybe I shouldn't have moved him, but the tide didn't give me much choice."

Ruth's stomach spasmed. "This is like some kind of horrible dream."

"So you didn't see him fall?" Jack pressed.

Roxie's eyes widened. "Look, Detective, I didn't do anything to this kid. I could have left him there to drown, but I didn't, so don't give me the third degree. It's called being a Good Samaritan, isn't it? I thought that was a good thing." She jammed her hands into her pockets. "Oh, I forgot about this."

She fished a small object from her pocket and gave it to Ruth. It was a fragment of shell about five inches long, pearly on the inside and the outer covering rough and dull colored. "It was in his hand when I found him. Weird."

"Why weird?" Ruth managed as she stared at the thing.

"He must have brought it with him or something because that's not from any kind of abalone I've ever seen."

Ruth squeezed the shard in her hand, too scared to speak, too overwhelmed to say anything. Visions of her boy swam before her eyes. Bryce, her baby, her son. "Please, God," she whispered. "Please help."

Jack pressed a hand to her shoulder. "Are you okay, Ruth?"

She shook her head. "I am going to be sick."

Jack ran to summon a nurse, and Roxie escorted Ruth to the bathroom, where she promptly threw up. Roxie helped her to the sink, and she got a good look at herself.

The terror had carved her face into an aged mask. She pressed a hand to her cheeks, wondering how much longer her legs would hold her up.

Roxie watched her in the mirror, her eyes bright with sympathy, her hands ready to catch Ruth if she faltered. "Can you make it back to the waiting room?"

"I'm not sure. My knees are awfully wobbly."

"Lean on me." Roxie put her shoulder under Ruth's and clasped a hand around her waist. She half escorted, half carried her out to a chair. The nurse went off to find a temporary room for Ruth. Jack brought her a cup of water. They stood, uncertain, watching her for a sign of what they should do next.

None of it seemed to touch Ruth. She was isolated, insulated, by a cloud of disbelief thick as Finny's springtime fog. The only sound that made a dent was the booming voice of Monk charging through Jack's phone line. The detective handed the cell over to her and moved a discreet distance away with Roxie.

"Ruthy? Jack told me. How is Bryce? I'm still stuck here because there's a whopper of a storm coming in. Oh, Ruthy, if I thought it would be any faster, I'd rent a car and drive, or even crawl on my hands and knees. Are you okay? I mean, health wise? Do you need to see a doctor?"

"I'm okay." Her voice sounded dull in her own ears. "Just sick. They're finding me a room to lie down."

"This is killing me, not being there with you. Is Bobby there? Is Jack staying with you?"

Ruth looked up to see Bobby just entering the building, a worried frown on her face. "She's here. They're all here. I'm perfectly fine. It's Bryce I'm not sure about.

He's got a bad head injury." Her voice broke.

"I know, honey, but he's a strong young man. Comes from good stock. He'll make it. I just know it."

It was exactly what she needed to hear. They talked for a long while; the anguish in his voice was clear.

"I'll be home just as soon as I can, Ruthy. I'll pray for Bryce. Mom and Dad will, too, and Dave. We're all going to pray like crazy for him and for you. I love you. I love you so much."

"I love you, too, Monk. Come home soon."

The doctor emerged a moment later with discouraging news. "He was hit with something, I'm fairly certain. The wound is too precise to have come from falling against those rocks. He has a skull fracture and significant swelling. We'll keep him in a medically induced coma to allow his body to rest. When the swelling subsides a little, we'll see if we can bring him out of it."

"If you can bring him out of it?" Ruth repeated, stupidly. "What happens if you can't?"

The man raised a hand to quiet her. "He's had a severe head injury. Nothing is guaranteed here. We'll have to take things one day at a time. That's the best I can do for now."

It seemed to Ruth that she'd been taking things one day at a time since the day she'd discovered she was pregnant. *I ought to be better at it by now.*

Dr. Ing was summoned to check on her. Bobby sat with her through the doctor's gentle poking and prodding. The sound of the babies' heartbeats reassured Ruth. He told her to get some rest, keep hydrated, and try to relax.

"That's a good one," she told Jack and Bobby as they rode home in Jack's car. "How can I relax? Someone tried to run me down, Paul is hurt, our house is broken into, and now Bryce." Her eyes pricked with tears. "I should be there, in the hospital. I should stay with my son."

Bobby squeezed her hand. "The doctor insisted you go home until morning. They'll call if there's any change at all. I'm going to stay with you every minute, and we'll pray together. Jack, Mary, and Nate are going to take shifts watching the house at night. Uncle Monk will be home as soon as he can. You need to take care of yourself and the babies."

She nodded, but the feeling of dread in her gut did not lessen.

"And if that isn't enough," Bobby said with a smile, "we can always go get Alva. He's ferocious with a baguette."

In spite of herself, Ruth smiled. "I guess it will be okay to go home for a little while."

They bundled her into the house.

Jack lingered in the kitchen after checking the house and grounds. Ruth surmised he was hoping to talk to Bobby alone, so she made herself scarce.

Jack's plan apparently did not pan out as she heard Bobby say, "Let's talk later. Now isn't a good time."

It is a good time, she wanted to tell the girl. She felt the urge to scream it at the top of her lungs. *Grab hold of love because it can be gone in a moment.* Sobs choked her throat. She went into the bathroom and turned on the bathtub taps for a good long soak. The running water covered the sound of her weeping.

Tucked into bed an hour later, her dreams were troubled,

vague images of cold water and suffocating darkness. Sleep eluded her for a long while until she did finally drop off into a fitful sleep.

The next morning she got up before dawn and quietly made tea, trying not to wake Bobby. She was halfway through her cup of decaf Earl Grey when she remembered the shell Roxie had given her. It was still in the pocket of her sweater. She laid it gently on the table, watching the play of colors in the fluorescent light. A picture of a sparkling walkway sprang into her mind. She could see them both in her imagination, Hui and Indigo feasting on Hang Town Fry, watching the sun electrify the treasures thrown up from the sea.

Bobby interrupted her thoughts, padding into the kitchen in a robe and slippers. "You're up early. Did you get any sleep?"

"Some." Ruth pushed the shell to her. It seemed so important somehow, to understand how the small piece wound up in her son's hand. Thinking of Bryce made her throat thicken, but she steeled herself against tears. She wouldn't do him any good if she turned into mush. "How could Roxie tell this abalone isn't from around here?"

Bobby peered at it. "It looks like a regular abalone shell to me. I'm better with land species than ocean life, I'm afraid. I was learning a lot from Ethan, but we didn't have a chance to complete our dives. Do you think it's a clue to who—" Her words trailed off.

"I don't know, but it's the only thing I can do to help him. Wait a minute." Ruth hurried to the shelf where she'd put the library books.

She grabbed the one entitled *Pacific Coast Ocean Life*.

There was a section on abalone, oysters, and mussels. Ruth read aloud about the five major species of abalone along the California coast.

"Did you know abalone come in designer colors?" Ruth squinted at the small print. "Black, white, green, pink, and red."

"I've never seen most of those types."

She read on. "That's because abalone is such a slow grower and reproducer. Indigo was right when she said their numbers were falling, and apparently we haven't done much to fix that problem since 1850. Look at this."

Ruth pointed to a section in bold print. "In California currently, all five major species of abalone are depleted."

Bobby picked up the shell and looked at it closely while Ruth continued to read. "People can still harvest red abalone, but they have to follow strict rules. Roxie was telling me about that. It is illegal to harvest white, green and pink and black at all. The white one is even on the endangered species list."

Bobby frowned. "You know, I've seen red abalone shells before and this one is different, now that I think about it." She turned it over and examined the other side. "Of course, we've only got a piece of it, but it's pretty high domed and small." She hefted it in her hand. "It's light, too, and the inside is silvery white rather than multicolored."

Ruth scanned down the page to a small picture. "Does it look like this one?"

They bent their heads together and held the fragment up to the tiny photo.

"Sure does to me." Bobby read the caption.

The both sat back in surprise.

Bobby was the first to break the silence. "The question is, considering they're nearly extinct, where did Bryce get a shell from a white abalone?"

~

They puzzled it over as they drove to the hospital for the second time that day. Bobby insisted that Ruth come home for a proper lunch and a nap after she sat with Bryce for several hours. Now her lunch sat precariously in her stomach as they returned. Ruth had an increasingly uneasy feeling. All of the frightening events from the past few months began to fit together. Who had an excellent knowledge of abalone, a connection to Reggie, and a definite need for money? She'd been so focused on the college people, she hadn't considered the other person who fit all the criteria: Roxie Trotter, the woman who found Bryce on the beach. She shared her thoughts with Bobby.

"It is mighty coincidental, but why did she bother bringing Bryce to the hospital? If she'd already murdered Reggie she couldn't have too much regard for the sanctity of life."

"Maybe she remembered how much it hurt to lose her son and she couldn't kill mine." The thought sent a ripple up Ruth's spine.

"And why bother running you down and breaking into the cottage? Doesn't seem like there's much for her to gain by that." Bobby drummed her fingers on the steering wheel. "I think we'd better talk to Jack about all this again. When is Uncle Monk coming back?"

"He finally got a three o'clock flight. Bubby Dean is

going to pick him up at the airport at six." She felt a surge of relief even saying the words aloud. Monk would be home soon. They would pick up the pieces of their crazy life and move on. He would be right by her side until Bryce recovered and help her figure out the whole rotten mess. She held onto that thought firmly as Bobby drove her to visit her son.

Her eyes flooded with tears again at the sight of him. He was pale, so pale, against the white of the pillows, his face swollen in its white wrappings. An IV tube curled around his arm, and a monitor recorded the steady beat of his heart.

In her mind she heard the tiny beating of her twins' hearts, and she held Bryce's hand. Her three children, her three precious blessings from God. She had made mistakes, no doubt, but sitting there with one hand on her abdomen and the other in Bryce's limp fingers, she knew. No one on earth could love these three children like she did. She would embrace even the smallest moment God gave her with them, and with His good grace they would live or die knowing that they were loved.

Tears flowed freely down her face as she pressed her cheek to his hand. "Lord, if it is Your will, help my son to heal. Help him to wake up and be there to love his new siblings. Help me to keep them all safe."

She closed her eyes imagining the sound of their heartbeats outside and within.

Alva woke her some hours later when he clanked his

toolbox down on the small table.

"Oh, sorry there," he stage whispered. "Didn't mean to startle ya. I figgered I'd just leave some candy for you and the buns in yer oven. The nurses said I shouldn't bring it in so I hadta hide it in a laundry bag. Nurses is kinda crabby sometimes. Must be from hanging out with all them sick people. Or maybe it's cuz they don't let 'em roller skate in the hallways. Hungry, sweet cheeks?"

"No, not really."

His forehead creased into a web of wrinkles. "Them babies might be up for a snack, though. You shouldn't deprive them of their sugar. They need to crystallize their bones and all that, otherwise they'll come out like rubber chickens."

She laughed. "You may be right about that. What do you have in your stash today?"

"Oh, the usual, only I scored some red licorice at the grocery. Can't chew it, though; sticks to my choppers."

She selected a crumpled bag of jelly beans and they sat down to nibble. Alva ate his chocolate bar with gusto while he stared at Bryce.

He tossed the wrapper in the trash and pointed a sticky finger toward the stricken man. "So, when you figger he's going to wake up?"

Tears crowded her eyes again. "He's been badly hurt, Alva. The doctor's aren't sure. . .if he is ever going to wake up."

Alva stared at her and then at Bryce. All at once he started to laugh. His chuckles grew louder and louder until tears ran down his face. "Those doctors is a hoot, ain't they? Of course he's a-goin' to wake up. Everybody wakes up, iffen not here then in heaven. The likes of them doctors. So many years in them fancy schools and they ain't learned a scootch." He wiped his eyes.

She looked in amazement at Alva, a nutty old man who in the oddest moments saw things with such clarity that it took her breath away. She found herself filled with happiness at sharing a moment with him. She reached a hand out to his. "You are a great friend, Alva, and a very wise man."

He grinned and tapped a finger to his temple. "That's on account of the preservatives in this candy. Keeps a brain sharp, you know."

A nurse poked her head in. "You aren't handing out candy, are you, Mr. Hernandez? I specifically told you not to do that."

He wiped a hand over his sticky mouth. "Who me? Nah. I'm just chatting is all." He winked at Ruth and lowered his voice as the nurse left. "I'd better go. Nurse Atilla there will take my treasures if I'm not careful." Alva dropped a kiss on Ruth's cheek and got up to leave.

An odd thought popped into Ruth's head. "Alva, will you do me a big favor?"

"Anything for you, sweet cheeks." He listened to her request and scuttled off, checking the hallway in both directions for the nurse before he ventured out.

J ack had an extra shot of coffee before he ventured to the hospital for the second time that day. He was terrified and elated at the same time. He knew it was wrong, with Bryce struggling to stay alive, but he also knew with a certainty that didn't visit him often that he was meant to share his life with Bobby. He had to tell her that he loved her, he had to ask her to stay. He'd waited far too long already.

He found her in the third floor waiting room.

"Bryce's condition hasn't changed," she told him. "Ruth has been sitting with him for hours. I'm worried about her."

"Should she go home and lie down?"

"I think so. I basically carried her out of here at lunchtime, but she wasn't having any part of it this time. She's got her mind fixed on figuring out who did this to him. As a matter of fact, Ruth and I have been concocting some wild theories that we figured we better share with you."

Noting the intensity on her face, Jack decided personal matters could wait a few more minutes. "You've got my undivided attention."

They sat, and Bobby filled him in on all things abalone.

Jack raised an eyebrow. "So you think that shell is the key to whoever attacked him?"

"Yes, crazy as it sounds. You don't look convinced."

"Oh, it's not that. Any theory is worth investigating

at this point, and Ruth has delivered up some oddball solutions to previous crimes that have proven to be spot on. I've got another angle I'm working on. As a matter of fact, I'm meeting someone later today who may shed some light on things."

"Good. We could use some light around here."

"That's for sure." He coughed and cleared his throat, shifting on the hard plastic chair.

She looked closely at him. "Are you okay? You look kind of pale."

"Yes, I'm fine." He took a deep breath and took her hand. "Bobby, I want to talk to you about something other than murder and mayhem."

Her black eyes were curious. "Shoot."

"I've had some time to think about what's important." His words died away as she waited. Again he sucked in a deep breath and exhaled to steady the spasms in his stomach. "It's been hard for me, after losing Lacey, to think about starting over, but here goes."

He looked into her earnest face and his heart melted again, filled with a warmth he was hopeless to describe. "I love you, Bobby. I've loved you from the moment I saw you. There is something about you that completes me, that gives me a reason to get up in the morning and fills a place in my heart that I didn't know was empty."

Her lips parted slightly. He thought he saw a sheen of moisture in her eyes.

Gaining courage, he forged ahead. "You are a huge part of my life and Paul's life, and I want you to stay here, to make a life with me." He waited, holding his breath.

She blinked. "Wow. I know how hard that was for

you to say, Jack. I'm kind of surprised. I mean, I really hoped to hear that for a long time, but I'd kind of decided I was never going to."

"I know. It shouldn't be a surprise, but I've been stupid, afraid to commit, afraid of investing in someone again. I'm sorry it took so long, Bobby, but I'm ready now."

"Oh, Jack. You are a wonderful man and a great father." She squeezed his hand for a long moment before she let it go. "But I can't stay."

His mouth fell open. "What? Why not? Because I've been such a clod?"

Her smile was wistful. "No, not that. Let me think how to say it."

She looked away for a moment, before her gaze returned to his face.

"It's because I don't think you're over your wife." She held up a hand when he started to protest. "I have to finish this. I think you convinced yourself you had a change of heart because I said I was leaving, not because you really wanted to commit."

She reached out a hand to stroke his cheek. "I love you, Jack. You are so special to me, and maybe someday we can start a life together if neither of us has gone in a different direction, but I'm not going to force you into that decision. That's not good grounds for a relationship."

He started to speak, but she cut him off.

"It's better this way, for both of us, and for your son. I'll be sure to say good-bye to him before I leave for Utah."

And she was gone.

Jack felt like he'd been hit with a two-by-four. He was

too weak to get up from the chair and go after her. His grand realization was too little, too late. Bobby was going to walk out of his life and Paul's and leave him with an aching hole in his heart. He'd finally messed things up so badly they couldn't be repaired.

His PDA beeped, reminding him of his appointment. The sound seemed far away, but it brought him back, at least enough for him to get to his feet. The pain in his gut did not lessen as he headed to the car. Why had he been such a fool? Bobby thought he was committing out of guilt, not out of love.

Maybe she was right. Was he really over Lacey? Did anyone ever really get over losing a spouse? Maybe he hadn't gotten over it, but he'd been able to move beyond, he was sure. He was ready to start a new phase, as Ruth had put it. He believed that with all his heart. It didn't matter, though, because Bobby didn't believe it. She would move on, find someone else, and he would see her only when she came to visit Monk and Ruth. Darkness gripped his insides.

The road north to Pacifica seemed endless. The surf thundered along Highway 1, mirroring his own inner turbulence. Another storm was rolling in along the water, dark clouds massing on the horizon. He could not keep his thoughts from Bobby, with her easy laugh and gentle smile. Bobby falling in love with someone else, making a life with another man.

It was after four before he pulled up at the small stucco house set apart from the road by a scruffy patch of lawn. Mr. Glenn greeted him with a smile and a hearty hug. "Well, hello there, Detective. Come to work on another merit badge?" The man's blue eyes sparkled from under white shaggy brows.

"No, Mr. Glenn. You made me do enough of those to earn my Eagle Award. I just had a question."

"A question for your old scoutmaster? I can't imagine what information you don't have access to in your line of work. Come in, let's get out of this wind."

They settled into a tiny living room. Mr. Glenn brought Jack a cup of coffee. "If you don't mind my saying so, you look a little down. Everything okay at work?"

"Oh, crazy as usual. Work is fine."

"And Paul?"

"He broke his wrist falling down the stairs. He's okay, but Louella is exhausted because she insists on holding his hand every time he goes up or down. I think the woman is about pooped out."

Mr. Glenn laughed. "Louella can handle it. I recall her managing a den full of ten-year-old boys without breaking a sweat."

"She could still do it, I'll bet." Jack put down his cup. "Anyway, that isn't why I came. I remembered something you taught us a long time ago about knot tying. Do you recall that project?"

"Of course. I also recall you and Nate tying up Roger so thoroughly we had to cut him out with a knife."

Jack laughed. "I blocked that out, I guess. I wonder if Roger has forgiven me."

"Probably. What can I do to help you?"

Jack slid the photo of the knot over to him. "Do you recognize this type of knot?"

"Hmmm. Let me see. I'm thinking it's a figure eight on a bight."

"That's what Ruth's husband thought, too, but he said

it isn't the kind of knot they used a lot on board his ship."

"I wouldn't think so. It's bulky and you need a lot of rope to tie it."

"Yes. That's why I came. I know it's a shot in the dark, but I wondered if you might know what kind of hobbyist or professional might use this knot?"

Mr. Glenn frowned. "Well, rock climbers, maybe." He winked at Jack. "Eagle Scouts, of course. That's about all I can think of."

Jack sat back feeling depleted. "We thought of the rock climbing angle, too. Nothing else comes to mind?"

"No, son, I surely wish I could be of more help, but the little gray cells aren't what they used to be."

"No problem." They chatted for a while until Jack excused himself. "It was good to see you. I guess I better be hitting the road before the rain comes in. Thanks, Mr. Glenn."

"Anytime, Jack." The man walked him to the car. Wind swirled the leaves of a nearby bank of eucalyptus. Jack started the car and was pulling away from the curb when he noticed Mr. Glenn waving at him.

He backed up and rolled down the window.

The man leaned down. "I just thought of something. There is one other type of person who might use a knot like that."

Jack's eyes widened as he listened. "Thanks so much, Mr. Glenn. I'll be in touch."

He hit the accelerator and took off for Finny.

~

Nate was waiting for him when he returned, the printout

in his hand. "You're right, but how did you figure it out?"

"I didn't. Mr. Glenn did."

"Scoutmaster Glenn? No way."

"Yes way."

"Did he make you whittle a spoon or something while you were there?"

"No." Jack's thoughts whirled. "It's the means, but what would the motive be?"

"That's the million-dollar question." Nate pulled on his mustache.

Jack's mind raced. "Could it have something to do with abalone?"

"What did you say?"

"Abalone."

The officer's face screwed up in confusion. "Why would somebody get murdered for abalone? They don't even make pearls."

"There are all kinds of treasure, my friend." Jack's thoughts turned to Bobby. He wondered if he'd lost his treasure forever.

Ruth held Bryce's hand, stroking it gently, willing the life back into it. The doctor explained that they were easing up on the medicine, hoping he would show signs of coming around. So far, she'd seen no movement but the rise and fall of his chest. Not the slightest hopeful twitch in the long hours she'd sat there. The clock read six fifteen. Monk's plane would touch down soon.

She got up to stretch her back muscles, shuffling around the small room cluttered with IVs and equipment of all sorts. The shell she'd asked Alva to deliver caught her eye again. She picked up the thing he'd pirated from the dentist's office and held it to the light along with the shard that Roxie had given her. She rubbed her tired eyes, but the strange similarity remained.

How could it be? It was impossible. She twisted and turned them both until her hands ached.

Bobby arrived with a cup of decaf for her. "Looking at those shells again?"

"I'm telling you, Bobby, they both came from the same type of animal. Look here." She handed them over.

Bobby held them close to her face. "I see what you mean, but how did Bryce get hold of a white abalone?"

"And how did Dr. Soloski? He said he bought it at a garage sale."

"It's possible, I suppose. Weird, but possible." Bobby's eyes moved along with her thoughts. "Whatever is going on around here, it all keeps coming back to the ocean."

"Mmm hmm." Ruth prowled around the tiny room some more trying to calm her jittery nerves. "I need to go for a walk on the beach. The walls are closing in. Will you go with me?"

"I would love to get some fresh air, but I don't think Jack or Uncle Monk would approve."

"I'll leave a message at home for Monk, and you can call and leave word for Jack at the station. He can come along if he'd feel better about it." Ruth thought she saw a wistful look on Bobby's face for a moment.

Ruth called home and Bobby reported Jack was on the road, so she left a voice mail on his cell phone.

"Okay, Aunt Ruth. Let's hit the beach before the sun goes down."

Ruth kissed Bryce on the forehead, and they headed out.

The tang of salt air revived them both. It was still warm, but a wind blew the surf into puffs of white cotton and sent the few tourists scuttling back to town for hot coffee. They wouldn't find it at Monk's. He'd insisted they close the shop for a few days so Bobby would be free to babysit Ruth. She wondered how they were going to afford all the baby gear that currently crammed her house from floor to rafters. Only a supreme act of will kept her from opening their credit card bill to assess the damage.

They stopped in the shelter of some rocks and stared at the turbulent ocean. Waves dashed against the wall of rock that curved out into the water. It formed a sheltered cove for swimmers and divers, but not today. It was deserted save for a lone bird, poking for one last meal before the sun set.

Ruth shivered.

"Cold?" Bobby asked.

"No. I was just remembering finding Reggie here." Her mind flashed back to the awful moment. Alva, Ellen, Dr. Soloski, even Roxie had all been witness to the terrible sight. She pulled her collar up around her chin.

"Ruth, look." Bobby pointed to a figure in a wet suit, climbing along the top of the rocky cliff. The person was silhouetted against the waning sun. "Isn't that—"

"Yes, it is. What is Dr. Soloski doing out here at this hour? What is he wearing? It couldn't be a wet suit."

"I'm going to go find out."

Ruth put a hand on her arm. "Oh, no, you don't. Those rocks are slippery, and Jack would most definitely not approve."

Bobby stiffened. "I'm just going to peek around the top and see where he's going, and I don't answer to Jack, by the way. I need to make a life without him." Her look softened and she kissed Ruth. "Stay here, and I'll be back in five minutes. Take my cell phone in case you need one."

Before Ruth could answer, Bobby was jogging up the beach toward the spot where Dr. Soloski had vanished over the top, after picking her way along the uneven path that led to the crest of the rock pile. Ruth tried to repress the anxious feeling in her gut by puzzling out the doctor's odd behavior.

Snatches of conversation played in her mind.

Ellen's grating voice. *"Do you dive, Doctor?"*

The doctor's reponse. *"No, ma'am. I'm a land creature all the way."*

So what was he doing heading into the surf wearing a wet suit? For a guy who was happiest in the trees, it didn't seem to fit.

The trees. A lightbulb flashed across her brain. He was an arborist, a person no doubt familiar with ropes—and all kinds of knots.

Take it easy, Ruth. The man is a dentist. He's from a wealthy family. Why would he want to kill Reggie? But he needed money. He'd told her how expensive the care was for his sister. Was he out looking for the White Queens, too? Had he encountered Reggie during the dive and murdered him?

It still made no sense, but Ruth's duty was clear. Even if it turned out to be her wild imagination at work, she had to get Bobby away from Dr. Soloski. With shaking fingers she dialed the police station, but the cliffs blocked the signal. She hastened a few steps onto higher ground with the same result. The cell phone was useless. There was no way to summon help except to return to town, and by that time it might be too late.

She peered once again at the black pile of rock. There was still no sign of Bobby. Ruth took off her hat and left the cell phone on a pile of rocks well away from the advancing tide. Then she set off for the cliff.

Jack listened again to the "signal unavailable" message on Bobby's cell phone before he clicked off his phone. His car engine idled outside the empty dentist office. He'd already checked the man's home with no luck. Ruth wasn't at the cottage or the hospital and neither was Bobby.

"Where is everybody?"

When his phone rang a second later he snatched it up. "Jack Denny."

"Where are they?" Monk bellowed. "Where are my wife and niece? The message on my machine says they went for a walk, but that was an hour ago. Do you have any ideas?"

Jack held the phone away from his ear. "I got the same message. Did she say where they went walking?"

"No, only that they went out for fresh air. Maude hasn't seen them, and Alva said they were at the hospital when Ruth asked him to bring his shell there, the one he boosted from the dentist. That's the last he's seen of her."

The shell? His suspicions were beginning to take on a more solid shade of black and white. "I'll check with the nurses and call you right back."

The nurse told him a minute later that they'd headed toward the beach. He dialed Monk again. "I'm going to pick you up. I think I know where they went."

Monk sighed. "Women. Why don't they ever stay where you tell 'em to?"

Jack didn't answer as he turned on the lights and siren and raced toward the cottage.

In five minutes Monk was strapping his big frame into the passenger seat. "What do you mean you think it was the dentist? Why would he kill Reggie? I thought the guy was well-to-do and all that. He's a professional man and all."

"I haven't figured out a motive yet. I may be totally wrong, but I did find out he is strapped for cash. His mother left everything in trust to the sick daughter and Soloski was left without a dime."

"Ouch."

"Yeah, but sister gets the bundle when she's twenty-one."

"Oh boy. I'll bet he's going to have her sign some papers on her birthday to give the wad to her loving brother, or—" Monk shot him a look. "Who gets the money if she dies?"

"Who do you think?"

"Uh-oh." Monk fisted his hands on his knees, his wide forehead bisected by creases of worry. "But really, Jack. What does it all have to do with Reggie?"

"I don't know, but Soloski needs plenty of income to pick up the tab on what insurance doesn't cover for his sister. His previous dental practice failed and left him near bankruptcy, but he's somehow been paying for her care all this time."

"So where's the cash coming from?"

"My question exactly."

Ruth watched the path carefully as she climbed the rocks. Inch by inch, the tide was filling in the cove far below. Getting past one more projection of rock should reveal Bobby's location. She carefully picked her way along and peeked around the black crag.

There was no one there. She looked in all directions for any sign of Dr. Soloski or Bobby. Where had they gone? If they'd climbed back down to the beach over the other side she would be able to see them on the ground below.

A sound made her turn.

"Hello, Ruth." Dr. Soloski's face was hard in the dusky light. His wet suit gave him an otherworldly appearance, as if he were a part of the rock from which he'd seemingly emerged.

Ruth tried to level her voice. "Oh, uh, Dr. Soloski. Where did you come from? I was, just, uh, looking for my niece."

He pointed to a crevice in the rock that she hadn't noticed before. It was virtually invisible, sheltered by a gnarled twist of black. "She's down there. Why don't you go join her?"

Ruth's breath grew shallow. Without taking her eyes off the dentist, she inched closer to the hole. "Bobby? Can you hear me?"

"She can't hear you." He smiled. "Too windy. Go on down and see her."

"I don't think—"

He grabbed her arm and propelled her toward the edge of the crevice. Her feet skidded on the wet rock. Soon she was forced down into the gap, scraping her elbows as she fought for balance. A rope ladder led down into blackness. Ruth looked at the man. "What will you do if I don't cooperate?"

His cruel smile told her the answer.

Feeling as though she'd stepped into a bad movie, she grasped the damp rope and climbed down.

Bobby lay at the bottom, bleeding from a cut on her head and chin. Ruth knelt next to her. "Oh Bobby, did he hurt you?"

"He shoved me and I fell. I think I broke my collarbone. I'm sorry, Aunt Ruth. I'm sorry I got us into this mess with Dr. Scary here."

"Shut up," Soloski said as he stepped off the ladder and joined them. "You've caused me no end of trouble. I'll have to harvest early now, and that cuts into my cash flow."

Though the dark walls seemed to close around her in a black fist, Ruth decided the best course of action was to try to stay calm and keep him talking. "Harvest what?"

Bobby pointed into the dark water that was now lapping over her shoes. She peered into the inky surface. Glimmers of white shone in the weak light. It clicked. White treasure, only a different kind than Señor Orson's pearls. "White abalone. You found a stash of white abalone, and you're poaching them."

"I wasn't looking for them. It was dumb luck really. But there they were one day when I was out on a dive avoiding your monstrous librarian. There they were, a treasure trove right under everyone's noses. The best ones are the deepest, eighty feet or so."

"But they're an endangered species. You might drive them into extinction." Ruth realized the stupidity of her statement as soon as she said it. "You don't care, do you? You killed Reggie because he stumbled onto your little business?"

He shrugged. "A minor glitch. He was a nobody. I didn't figure anyone would be nuts enough to be in the ocean at night. That's when I harvest. The camera guy must have been a nut because there he was, swimming up from the lower vent. I suppose I should have handled it better, but I was so surprised I just dropped the rope over his neck and strangled him. More instinct than anything else. Your son was a bigger problem. He saw me heading out of my hidey hole. I tripped and one of the abalone fell out of the bag and smashed." He shook his head. "Such a waste. Anyway, your nosy son was right there to see it all, so I had to disable him."

Ruth was overwhelmed with rage. "Disable him? You could have killed him. All to make a few bucks."

"More than a few. My buyers will pay two hundred dollars each for these babies, the big ones anyway, plus a nice bonus for the trouble I take to smuggle them out of here. I've already sold almost five hundred of them and I figure I can scrape another five hundred or so before the lot is depleted. I ship the shells overseas and get a nice bit for those, too, before they're made into cheap jewelry or whatever."

He smiled in satisfaction. "All things considered it's enough to cover my expenses, at least until my beloved sister turns twenty-one next month. The abalone supply should hold out until then. When Mommy Dearest's trust fund kicks in, I won't ever need to sell another thing as long as I live."

Ruth's feet felt chilled to the bone as the water lapped her ankles. "Maude thought you were wealthy."

He laughed. "The old prune. She would believe anything, as long as it came from the mouth of an eligible man."

Bobby groaned. "Why did you come to Finny anyway?"

"I came to this nowhere town to escape some creditors. There isn't exactly a wealth of patients here so I had plenty of time to check out the beach. While I was diving one day, I noticed there is a vent along the cliff side about fifty feet down, so I dove to check it out, and bingo. I didn't know they were white abalone at first. I'd have been happy to poach any kind, really. Lucky they were a rare type. Restaurateurs will pay extra for them."

"And you said you didn't dive," Ruth said bitterly.

"I said a lot of things you bought, hook, line, and sinker."

"So why did you try to run her down and break into the house?" Bobby said, her voice thin. "Was there any particular reason for that?"

"I saw her at the library researching, and she had the shell that idiot Alva took from my office. I wanted to get it back, or discourage her from doing any more poking around."

"You are insane," Bobby said.

His smile shone white in the dark. "Insanely rich, soon. Rich people are forgiven all their little foibles." He glanced at the water. "The tide's coming in. I've got to go and be prepared to be suitably grieved when your bodies wash up on the beach."

Ruth fought a swell of panic. "You can't leave us here to die."

Dr. Soloski began to climb the rope ladder. "I could kill you first, if you'd like. I'm pretty good with knots." His laughter echoed through the cavern as he ascended and pulled the rope ladder up in his wake.

She could not restrain a shriek of abject terror as the ladder slithered upward and disappeared. The only sound was the rush of surf filling in the rock tunnel and then retreating, each time bringing the frigid water a few inches higher.

Ruth tried to move Bobby to a drier spot, but she resisted.

"Just help me up. We've got to get out of here."

Wondering how that was going to be possible, she hooked a shoulder under Bobby's arm and pulled her to a standing position.

The girl grimaced, leaning unsteadily against the rock,

the water now up to their knees.

"Can we climb out?" Ruth peered upward into the circle of sky that was now a deep pearly gray, thick with clouds.

"I don't see how. The rocks are sheer and even if we did he might be waiting at the top. Did you call Jack before you came to get me?"

Her heart constricted. "Yes, but there was no signal."

Bobby put her arm around Ruth and chafed her shoulders. "It's not good for the babies to have your body temperature drop."

Ruth's smile was grim. "It's not going to be good for them when I drown, either."

The circle of freezing sea water had reached her waist. She tried to climb up higher on the rocks to keep her stomach out of the wet, but her feet couldn't get a purchase on the slippery rock. "You're right, there's no way to climb up and no one will hear us if we scream." The panic had now morphed into a numb blanket of terror that wrapped around her insides and seemed to squeeze the breath out of her.

Bobby looked into the dark expanse of water. "Then we'll have to go down."

Ruth wondered if perhaps Bobby hit her head in the fall. "What?"

"Aunt Ruth, listen to me carefully because we don't have much time. Dr. Soloski is right, there's a vent below us. I'd say it's probably twenty feet down from where we are standing. It connects this tunnel to the ocean. That's how the good doctor gets in and out at high tide."

"What are you saying, Bobby?" There was a frantic edge

in Ruth's voice as the water crept toward her shoulders.

"We've got to dive down and swim to that opening and out into the cove. If it's big enough to fit the doctor in scuba gear, and Reggie, then we can fit, too."

Ruth's eyes widened. "I can't do that. I'm not even a good swimmer when there aren't waves and slippery rocks and two babies inside me."

"Stick close to me and I'll try to pull you along, but once we're out in the ocean you've got to make for shore. I'm going to be slow, so you just get out as fast as you can."

Her head whirled. "Bobby, you might drown. We both will probably drown. This is crazy. Maybe we should wait for help."

Bobby's black hair formed a helmet around her face. She pointed to the water that lapped her chest. "Aunt Ruth, we're going to drown right here, right now, or die of hypothermia. It's the only way out. Can you do it?"

No, her mind screamed. Dive into that freezing blackness and hope for a hole to squeeze through? She could not do that, it was too much. But how could she not give the babies that chance? How could she decide for them that they would all drown in this horrible cave and never see the precious light of day? How could she end their lives before they'd felt their father's caress or seen the love in their parents' eyes?

She thought about Monk, who would be mad with worry, and Bryce, who would have no one to wake up for if they died. She reached out a hand to Bobby. "Father God," she said, "give us the strength to fight for our lives. Help us to find our way back to the people who love us, if that is Your desire, and give us peace to accept Your will if it is not."

Bobby squeezed her frozen fingers. "I love you, Aunt Ruth. We're going to make it."

"I love you, too, Bobby." She took a shaky breath. "The babies are getting cold. Let's dive."

⚊

The dark feeling in Jack's stomach increased with each mile. He radioed the station to arrange for backup and a fire department response. Coast Guard, too, though they would not arrive for a half hour or so.

They'll be fine. We'll probably meet them walking back from the beach. Something told him it was not true. They pulled off as near the sand as they could get. Nate screamed in behind them, flashers still going. Half skidding, half jogging, they made it to the gravel trail.

"Look," Monk cried. He held up Ruth's hat and the phone. "She left them here for us to find. I know it."

Dr. Soloski emerged out of the darkness. He froze for a moment, his eyes taking in the three men. Then he took another step toward them.

"I was coming to get help. It's Bobby and Ruth. They were up walking along the rocks and the tide came it. I tried to get to them, but the surf is too rough."

Monk took one look at the man, and then he was on him like a mountain lion. His hands fastened around Soloski's throat over the rubberized wet suit. "My aunt Petunia's bonnet, you were trying to get help. What did you do with them?" His roar made the doctor flinch.

"I don't know what you're talking about," Dr. Soloski

gasped. "I was trying to save them."

Jack and Nate tried to pull Monk's hands away.

Jack felt the desperation well up inside him. "We know you killed Reggie. Don't compound your crimes here by adding two more lives."

"Four," Monk said, savagely. "Don't forget Ruth's got twins on board."

The prone man gave Jack a look that showed for the briefest of seconds the wickedness under the veneer of gentility. "You've got no proof of anything, and if I were you, I wouldn't waste time with accusations when two women are probably drowning right this minute."

"Where are they?" Jack shouted.

Soloski only laughed.

Monk let go as if he'd been burned and ran on toward the surf. Jack followed, leaving Soloski for Nate to handcuff.

They raced along over the shifting pebbles. The outline of the rock pile was silhouetted against the last rays of sun. Waves crashed against the wall, sending arms of foam clear to the top.

Jack stared desperately, trying to pick out any sign of Bobby or Ruth. The narrow path that joined the beach to the cliffs was already underwater. "Bobby!" he shouted. "Ruth! Where are you?"

The wind flung the words back at him.

Monk's face was stark with terror. "I don't see them. Where are they?"

Both men turned their faces to the dark, heaving water. After a split second, Monk stripped off his shoes and Jack followed suit. The freezing water swirled around their knees. Then the sound of a motor cut through the night.

Roxie aimed a light at them from her motorboat. "Get in. I can take you close. I know these rocks."

Monk didn't hesitate. He splashed out to the boat and Roxie helped him in before they both gave Jack a hand up.

She steered the vessel out into the choppy surf. "I heard your call on my police radio. Where do you think they were?"

Jack pointed to the rocky crag. "Soloski said they were walking along the cliffs. He must have disabled them somehow."

Roxie shook her head as they boat chugged through the choppy waters. "I knew there was something wrong about him."

Jack wished with all his power that he had realized the truth earlier.

As the salt spray stung his eyes, he wondered if his error would cost four lives.

<hr>

The ice cold water swallowed Bobby in a moment. Ruth waited for one second more, sucking in as much precious air as she could before she let go of the jagged rocks and swam after her.

Her belly interfered with her downward progress, forcing her to grab onto rocks to pull herself farther into the abyss. Though her eyes burned, she didn't dare take them off Bobby for an instant. She knew it must be excruciating for the woman to make any progress with a broken collarbone.

Ruth's lungs ached as the darkness increased along with her panic. If they didn't reach the vent soon—

Something tugged at her pants, arresting her progress. She yanked the fabric loose from where it had snagged on a sharp rock. When she looked up again, Bobby was gone.

She frantically scanned in all directions, but there was nothing but black.

The facts settled around her like iron weights. She was going to die in darkness along with her babies. The only thing she could feel was the cold, settling into her very core. She couldn't move. Even the tiny kicks from inside had stilled.

"God deliver us," she prayed as Indigo had so many years before in the grip of a violent ocean.

A glimmer of white caught her eye in the gloom. The abalone, clustered in a great wide band, lay like a pearl necklace against the rock. Knowing she had only seconds of air left, Ruth scooted along the trail of domed creatures, ignoring the cut of their barnacle-encrusted shells on her fingers.

Lungs screaming, eyes half closed, she saw it: an irregular circle cut into the rock.

The vent that led out to the sea.

"There," Monk shouted. He pointed to a bit of yellow on the swirling surf. He dove in. Roxie and Jack waited, bent over the side, until Monk dragged the bundle to the side.

Monk cradled Ruth in his arms on the bottom of the boat. Her eyes were closed, but she breathed. "She's alive." Monk's face was torn with emotion. "She's alive, praise the holy Father and His loving Son. She's alive."

Jack returned to the side and continued to scan.

Roxie played the light across the surface of the water. Nothing.

Teeth clenched, every nerve on fire, he scanned left and right, left and right.

The tiniest flash of white caught his eye. He didn't think twice before he was in the water. The cold hit him like a slap, but he swam against the strong pull of the surf until he reached her.

Bobby floated facedown in the water, hair fanned out in the surf.

He flipped her over and started swimming with all his might toward the boat.

Waves pushed against him, crashing over his head.

He fought against the relentless power of the sea until he reached the pitching vessel.

Roxie and Monk lifted them back in.

Jack laid Bobby on the deck. Her face was deathly pale, tinged with blue. He held his cheek to her mouth.

"She's not breathing." He unzipped her jacket and tilted her chin back.

Roxie's face was grim. She took her fingers from the girl's neck. "No pulse. I know CPR. I'll do the compressions." She began to push on Bobby's chest in a steady rhythm that defied the rocking of the deck beneath them.

Vaguely Jack felt the boat move as Monk steered it back toward land.

He put his mouth onto Bobby's cold lips and blew, willing his life to mingle with hers and bring her back to him.

Ruth pulled the blankets around her, even though the hospital room was a toasty temperature. She felt as if she'd never be fully warm again. Monk opened the blinds to let in the morning sunshine. He kissed her on each cheek and her forehead.

"How are you feeling today?"

"Okay. How are you? Sleeping in a chair can't be too comfortable."

He rolled his big shoulders. "I didn't sleep much anyway. Mostly I just watched you."

Her cheeks warmed. "That must have made for a long night."

His eyes gleamed with moisture. "I could watch you every minute of every day and be a perfectly happy man."

She steadied her breath, luxuriating again at the simple blessing of being able to inhale and exhale. "How is Bryce?"

"The doctor says he's showing encouraging signs of coming around. We'll have to be patient and pray."

She laughed. "God has had an earful from me already."

"Me, too, but He's a great listener."

Jack knocked gently. "Mind if we come in?"

"Not at all." Monk moved to the other side of the bed to accommodate Bobby's wheelchair.

Ruth noted the pallor of Bobby's face and the sling holding her shoulder steady, but there was something else about her that made Ruth take notice: a calm and a contentment that she had not seen in the young woman before.

Jack kept his hand on Bobby's good shoulder as he talked. "How are you doing, Ruth? We were worried there for a while."

"So was I, but the doctor was able to stop the contractions. I'm on bed rest until further notice. What happened to the awful dentist?"

"He's been arrested for the murder of Reggie and the attempted murder of you two lovely ladies and your son. There will be more charges relating to poaching and such, but that will get us started."

Ruth watched the way Bobby reached up to cover Jack's hand with hers. She smiled. "Will you be postponing taking that job in Utah?"

"Yes. I think I'm going to stay here and hang out with this big lug. Almost drowning kinda put a new spin on things for me."

Ruth shivered. "I'll never swim in the ocean again."

Bobby laughed. "I don't have any choice. Jack needs to learn how to dive so he can keep the eyes of law enforcement on those abalone, or what's left of them."

They chatted for a while until Bobby showed signs of tiring and Jack wheeled her back to her room. Monk went off to fetch a cup of tea for his wife.

Ruth settled into the beam of sunlight that played across the bed. How very blessed she felt to be alive, and warm and surrounded by people she loved. The babies kicked and rolled inside her. She knew they would be okay, growing and thriving with parents who loved them desperately.

From her window she could just make out the silvery rise and fall of the ocean. She marveled at all the treasures it contained.

God saved me with His white treasure, Indigo said of the small bit of flour that ensured her survival.

Had He done the same with Ruth? Provided a path of silvery white abalone to guide her home?

She smiled, feeling the babies rollicking inside her, and turned her face to the sun.

Dana Mentink lives in California with her husband and two children. Her first love is the classroom; she has taught children from preschool through fifth grade for over a decade.

Dana is perpetually in search of a great story, either through painfully expensive trips to the bookstore or via her own labors in front of the computer. She enjoys writing cozies for Heartsong Presents—MYSTERIES! as well as suspense stories.

In addition to her novels, Dana writes short articles, both fiction and nonfiction, for a wide variety of magazines. Dana enjoys mentoring other writers and finding new vehicles to provide her readers with a hefty dose of mystery, merriment, and make-believe. Contact Dana on her Web site: www.danamentink.com.

You may correspond with this author by writing:
Dana Mentink
Author Relations
PO Box 721
Uhrichsville, OH 44683

A Letter to Our Readers

Dear Reader:
In order to help us satisfy your quest for more great mystery stories, we would appreciate it if you would take a few minutes to respond to the following questions. We welcome your comments and read each form and letter we receive. When completed, please return to:

Fiction Editor
Heartsong Presents—MYSTERIES!
PO Box 721
Uhrichsville, Ohio 44683

Did you enjoy reading *Treasure Under Finny's Nose* by Dana Mentink?

Very much! I would like to see more books like this! The one thing I particularly enjoyed about this story was:

_____

_____

_____

Moderately. I would have enjoyed it more if:

_____

_____

_____

Are you a member of the HP—MYSTERIES! Book Club?
Yes   No

If no, where did you purchase this book?

_____

Please rate the following elements using a scale of 1 (poor) to 10 (superior):

___ Main character/sleuth   ___ Romance elements

___ Inspirational theme   ___ Secondary characters

___ Setting   ___ Mystery plot

How would you rate the cover design on a scale of 1 (poor) to 5 (superior)? _____

What themes/settings would you like to see in future **Heartsong Presents—MYSTERIES!** selections? _____

_____

_____

_____

Please check your age range:
- ○ Under 18   ○ 18–24
- ○ 25–34   ○ 35–45
- ○ 46–55   ○ Over 55

Name: _____

Occupation: _____

Address: _____

E-mail address: _____

COZY IN KANSAS

THREE ROMANCE MYSTERIES

NANCY MEHL

Mystery, love, and inspiration in a small town bookstore. College student Ivy Towers has definite plans for her future. But when her great-aunt Betty is found dead inside her rare bookstore, Ivy must travel back to a place and a past she thought she'd left behind. She discovers that Bitty's supposed fall from her library ladder seems quite suspicious. Ivy's decision to poke her nose into things changes her destiny and propels her into uncovering carefully hidden secrets buried deep below the surface in the small town of Winter Break, Kansas. Along the way, she will discover that love can be found where you least expect it—and in the most mysterious of circumstances.

ISBN 978-1-60260-228-1
$7.97

Available wherever books are sold.

Heartsong Presents

Any 8 Titles
for $32!
A 20%
Savings!

Great Mysteries at a Great Price! Purchase Any Title for Only $4.97 Each!

HEARTSONG PRESENTS—MYSTERIES!
TITLES AVAILABLE NOW:

___MYS1 *Death on a Deadline*, C. Lynxwiler, J. Reynolds, S. Gaskin

___MYS2 *Murder in the Milk Case*, C. Speare

___MYS3 *In the Dead of Winter*, N. Mehl

___MYS4 *Everybody Loved Roger Harden*, C. Murphey

___MYS5 *Recipe for Murder*, L. Harris

___MYS6 *Mysterious Incident at Lone Rock*, R. K. Pillai

___MYS7 *Trouble Up Finny's Nose*, D. Mentink

___MYS8 *Homicide at Blue Heron Lake*, S. P. Davis & M. E. Davis

___MYS9 *Another Stab at Life*, A. Higman

___MYS10 *Gunfight at Grace Gulch*, D. Franklin

___MYS11 *A Suspicion of Strawberries*, L. Sowell

___MYS12 *Murder on the Ol' Bunions*, S. D. Moore

___MYS13 *Bye Bye Bertie*, N. Mehl

___MYS14 *Band Room Bash*, C. Speare

___MYS15 *Pedigreed Bloodlines*, S. Robbins

___MYS16 *Where the Truth Lies*, E. Ludwig & J. Mowery

___MYS17 *Fudge-Laced Felonies*, C. Hickey

___MYS18 *Miss Aggie's Gone Missing*, F. Devine

___MYS19 *Everybody Wanted Room 623*, C. Murphey

___MYS20 *George Washington Stepped Here*, K. D. Hays

___MYS21 *For Whom the Wedding Bell Tolls*, N. Mehl

___MYS22 *Drop Dead Diva*, C. Lynxwiler, J. Reynolds, S. Gaskin

___MYS23 *Fog Over Finny's Nose*, D. Mentink

___MYS24 *Baker's Fatal Dozen*, L. Harris

___MYS25 *Treasure at Blue Heron Lake*, S.P. Davis & M.E. Davis

___MYS26 *Everybody Called Her a Saint*, C. Murphey

___MYS27 *The Wiles of Watermelon*, L. Sowell

___MYS28 *Dog Gone!*, E. Key

___MYS29 *Down Home and Deadly*, C. Lynxwiler, J. Reynolds, S. Gaskin

___MYS30 *There Goes Santa Claus*, N. Mehl

___MYS31 *Misfortune Cookies*, L. Kozar

___MYS32 *Of Mice. . .and Murder*, M. Connealy

___MYS33 *Worth Its Weight in Old*, K.D. Hays

___MYS34 *Another Hour to Kill*, A. Higman

___MYS35 *Treasure Under Finny's Nose*, D. Mentink

___MYS36 *Kitty Litter Killer*, C. Speare

(If ordering from this page, please remember to include it with the order form.)

MYSTERIES!

Heartsong Presents—MYSTERIES! provide romance and faith interwoven among the pages of these fun whodunits. Written by the talented and brightest authors in this genre, such as Christine Lynxwiler, Cecil Murphey, Nancy Mehl, Dana Mentink, Candice Speare, and many others, these cozy tales are sure to challenge your mind, warm your heart, touch your spirit—and put your sleuthing skills to the test.

Not all titles may be available at time of order.
If outside the U.S., please call
740-922-7280 for shipping charges.